MASCARA

Book 1

A. PALASCIANO

A PERSONAL THANK YOU

I would like to thank my family first and foremost for their continued support through my journey and for a childhood address right behind a public library.

I would also like to thank my fiancé Kevin for his support up and down the manic roller coaster called artistry. I'd like to thank my step-daughter to-be Olivia, for consulting with me on teenage behaviors today.

I would like to thank Gene Ritchings for his editing eye and TBishPhoto for their picture perfect know-how.

I want to thank the many amazing people who helped me print this book: Colleen Simmons, Brian Witte, Lisa Illions Forlenzo, Desmond Phillips, Evan Meszaros, Danielle Amato, Marjorie "Jorie" Kaplan, Lyana Medric, Angela Cuidera, Jason Little, Natalie Forte, Greg Peterson, Chagnon Earley, Sara Noce, Cara Palasciano, Elihn Glass, Michelle Minster, Marie & Tony Palasciano, Barbara Pereda, Sarah Little, Patrick Halm, Melissa Strignile Warcholik, Tania Isley-Robinson, Stephanie Kurilla, Arlene Fraser, Adam Marinos, Sharon Grant, Kara Doyle, Maria Donato, Susie Sehulster, Rich Beshada, Margie Gilbert & Dru Whitacre, Michael Favata, Ashley Stimson, Louise Wegrzyn, Stacy Smith, Tara Briley, Jessica Angelo, Donna Pizzulli, Pamela de Waal, Tracy Jerue, Katie Megill, Jen Rothacker, Kevin Goodrich, Holly Corbett, Jennifer Ferrara, Frank & Mary Ann Guerriero, Maryann Mueller, Jaime Dorishook, Melissa Lloyd, Gina Lutkus Naso, Stephanie O'Connell, Rachel Wagner, Nicole Trollo, Alison

Holland, Wes Denton, Kristina Bannon, Allan Zuniga, Kathy Colon, Desiree Meek, Heather Andrews, Tracy & Scott Hearon, Tommy & Kathy Reid, Emily Schoener, Jessica Dure, Julie Carlson, Marie Stinson, Robyn Herman, Tara & Matt Kocen, Tammy Lombardo, Jessica Levine, Sharon Malenda, Takreem Russo, Thomas Ascough, Jason Morcilio, Billy Purnell, Monica Caamano, Kim Linane, Michele Palomba, Violet Fournier, Maria Mattera, and Jeffrey Wong.

Lastly, I'd like to thank my real life lying/backstabbing frenemy who stole my friends (you know who you are), my private high school, and my college sorority for the inspiration behind this book.

CHAPTER 1

"Asher Sutherland"

Cobalt blue. That's how it starts.

That's how everything starts. With a color that most people think is only the name of some metal. Because most people, most *normal* people anyway, don't revolve their lives around a color. Or a tube of make-up. Or an indie band cover of Folsom Prison Blues for that matter.

But, I'm not normal. I never really thought I was. And the elitist crowd of Saint Lawrence Academy?

Definitely not normal.

I can tell you a couple pieces of fact I am sure of:

- My name is Jorie Carr. I am in my fourteenth year on this planet.
- Two months ago, I had an unopened package of mascara taped to my locker. Literally.

- In the right corner of the mascara package where companies like to put starbursts of high-impact ads it said, *Cobalt Blue*, to tell you the color.
- The tape was blue painter's tape, cut into perfectly even strips that went all around the four sides of the packaging.
- I had only really worn mascara like six times in my life before that day.
- Cobalt blue mascara will likely change the course of my life forever.
- I am one hundred percent serious.

Have you ever known someone or a few "someones" who were just made of perfect? Male, female, didn't matter. Either way, something about them, "je ne sais quoi" they call it in French, just acts as a magnet to everyone around them? Like cat nip.

In high school, there are always a handful of these flawless near-mythical creatures. Beautiful young Charles Mansons they are. Faces like they've been airbrushed but insides like dictators. Everything they do is magic.

You can't help but follow these kinds of people. There is just this thing, this thing that can't be described. Their movements, the way their hair falls, their laugh, their penmanship...

It's crack. You want to know them and you want to be seen knowing them.

The first near-mythical creature I had ever encountered in the land of high school was Asher Sutherland. *Asher Sutherland*. Even her name was cool.

Mine? Oh right you may have thought mine was cool too. Except Jorie stands for Marjorie and what decent parent names their kid Marjorie if it's not 1948?

To make matters worse, I got called "Marjorie Carjorie" all throughout grade school. So I finally went by Jorie Carr much to the disagreement of my birth certificate.

Asher Sutherland on the other hand? Born Asher Renee Sutherland. No childhood ridicule or poor man's rhyme inspiring her non-name-change name change.

I first encountered Asher in lunch, my very first week at Saint Lawrence Academy.

It was September, just after Labor Day, which I *always* spend at this beach house that my parents have in Long Beach Island, NJ. I had spent a relaxing weekend with my mom and younger brother, Matt, catching fish and final minutes of sunshine.

My dad was away on business, this time in Tulsa, which was fine by me. I knew he'd been struggling lately with the fact that I was about to start high school. He asked all sorts of awkward dad questions. Most of the time he started the questions and then stopped mid-sentence because he wasn't even sure if he wanted to know the answer.

The first day at Saint Lawrence was the Tuesday that followed my relaxing weekend at the beach. It was the last weekend that I really truly knew myself, or this prior version of myself, only I didn't know that then.

I was just two weeks shy of turning 14 and I'd had the same friends since I was basically four. Neighbors that became friends, friends that became like family. But I had outgrown them in a way. Not that I didn't want to be friends with them anymore, but something.

Something made me want to go to Saint Lawrence Academy and meet new kids that I hadn't known since I was four. Now, you're probably thinking it was the Marjorie Carjorie thing, but it wasn't. I'd been Jorie since 4th grade and things were, well, fine.

Just fine.

Until one day they weren't fine and I was plain old good and bored with everyone I knew. There was also a cute boy (understatement of the year) that I knew was attending Saint Lawrence.

Only one of *my* actual friends was going to Saint Lawrence: Abby Port.

Abby's mom and my mom were friends since high school. We lived right next door to each other. My mom and Abby's mom had planned on us being friends before we were even born, so really, I didn't have a say in the matter.

Every Friday night, my mom and Abby's mom drank at least two bottles of wine between them. My dad always stayed late at the store my family owned on Friday nights.

My mom and Abby's mom would act like it was a surprise decision to drink two bottles of wine, one they mulled over all week. But they weren't kidding anyone. Two bottles of cheap Pinot Noir (Pee No New Are) were set on my counter every Friday afternoon in anticipation and in recycling empty by Saturday morning in shame.

Usually, they'd eat some kind of trendy cheese or sugary dessert and laugh until they snorted. Then would come the cackle, a dance move no one should ever do, and then they'd become sullen for a while starting with the "remember that time" thought train.

"Remember that time when we saw blah blah blah

and you blah..."

Something like this.

Mom would be passed out within a half hour of when the "remember that time" train departed.

But I digress.

Abby and I both probably saw Saint Lawrence Academy as a way to do more with our lives than wind up exactly like our mothers in twenty years.

So on the afternoon of September 8th, there we were, desperate to meet new people and yet clinging to each other when we walked into fourth period lunch like two lost leeches reunited.

The room was just so, ginormous. There may have been a thousand students in that lunchroom. I never counted, but every day still, I am tempted to.

We found an eighth of a table that was open and hunkered down with all of our bags and books and disarray.

"Who did you get for history?" Abby asked.

"Walsh. You?" I remembered.

"Nicholson. What about chemistry?"

"Desoto."

And then I saw her. Out of the corner of my eye at first, and then I had to turn my whole head. It was just impossible not to.

Carrying a tray with one single balanced yogurt and a Styrofoam bowl of cafeteria fruit was a girl with long dirty blond curls, breasts impossible for high school and blue eyelashes. Not like, "maybe her eyelashes are blue" blue, but undoubtedly the brightest, poppiest blue you've ever seen.

Asher Sutherland.

I've never stared at a girl like I did in that moment. Abby stared too. I'm fairly certain the entire lunch room stopped, mid-chew, and stared at Asher Sutherland from the second she entered the room until the second she left, the freshmen in a "who was that girl" way and everyone else in a "there's Asher stop what you're eating" kind of way.

Looking back now, my naiveté to the entire MASCARA phenomenon was like a baby with its first set of blocks.

These look enchanting and foreign to me. Pretty blocks...

So there I was, smack in the middle of my first day at Saint Lawrence picturing a baby and a haphazard set of first blocks, stupefied by Asher

Sutherland and completely un-introduced to MASCARA, most likely looking like a drugged and drooling patient, when she spoke to me.

To clarify, I'm not a lesbian. Neither is Abby. And yes, I think one knows these things this early on. I didn't have a laundry list of boyfriends to speak of, but I had had a boyfriend before, and boys perplexed me in a way that I knew was par for the straight course.

In other words, I liked them, most of them, *a lot*. I crushed over a new boy every month but kept most of my crushes to myself. Like Joe, the guy I kind-of-sort-of came to Saint Lawrence for. "For" is a strong word. More like, the seed was planted by (cute is an understatement boy) Joe.

Bottom line? I found boys endlessly intriguing, their puzzling ways and fumbling coming of age.

"Coming of age" was a phrase I had heard my mom say before and I know that fourteen or so isn't the age, but my God were they buffoons, awkwardly turning into their own selves and trying desperately to be manly.

Buffoons, by the way, is my favorite word.

So all of this nonsense was unraveling around spools of deep and cliché thought when Asher Sutherland spoke to me.

"Hi. What's your name?" was the perfectly annunciated, swimmingly thought-out phrase that left her might-as-well-have-had-surgery lips.

What's my name? What is it? Why don't I know my own name?

"Jorie Carr, I'm a freshman," I leaked.

Why did I just tell her I am a freshman? She didn't ask what grade I'm in. Ugh. I hate myself.

Abby stood wide-eyed and feeling sympathy pains for my diarrhea of the mouth.

Asher laughed this laugh that was near-scripted in length and volume. I could smell her hair. It smelled like coconut and perfect. Whatever that smelled like.

"Of course you're a freshman. You're adorable. 'Jorie.' Is that your real name? I've never heard it before," said Asher freaking Sutherland. To me.

Is that my real name? How does she know? Ridiculously perfect looking and psychic. Folks, it's the all-knowing Asher Sutherland!

This crowd applauds in my head like they did for Houdini once upon a time, and I am so distracted that again, I probably looked challenged while she was speaking to me.

"Well," I stuttered.

I played the "Marjorie Carjorie" song from fourth grade in my head.

"It's a long story," is what I said.

Abby piped in, "It's short for Marjorie." She said it so fast it sounded like one word, like "itsshortformarjorie."

Thank you Abby who just spilled my adolescent secrets like a careless glass of milk.

I tried not to hate my friend in this very crucial moment.

"Marjorie. Really?" Asher said, then asked.

I was backed in to a corner. Betrayed by the only human I knew here. Like Abraham in the Bible. Was that even right?

"Yes," I reluctantly offered.

"What a lovely name," Asher said.

I remember it like song lyrics.

What a lovely name.

Marjorie? Lovely for who, your grandmother?

"Thank you," I said.

With that, Asher smiled and walked away, the back of her hair forever etched in my now-spinning mind – those long locks of blond that looked like her blow dryer woke her up in the morning, kissed her, and told her the cartoon birds would handle the rest. My blow dryer instead had this long drawn out argument with me every morning, basically telling me "shaving your head would be better."

"That's crazy huh," Abby had said.

I chewed, because now and only now could I finally eat.

"What is?" I asked with a mouth full of French fries.

"Haven't you heard yet about MASCARA?" Abby asked.

"Like the crap you put on your eyes? I have, I just never seem to get it to look that good and—"

"No Jorie, the clique, MASCARA."

"Clique?" Was this a new brand of make-up? I thought it was pronounced Clin-ique. Shows what I know.

"MASCARA is, like, the school sorority. It stands for Mara, Asher, Sue, Carmen, Amanda, Rachel and I think, Adrianna. I heard about them in first period. I thought for sure you already knew."

I chewed. She had spit out their names like they were her on last period class test.

"Asher runs the thing, kind of like she runs the school. Student Council President meets homecoming queen," said Abby.

I continued to chew.

"They all wear this blue mascara and they basically control everything," she continued. "Some girl, Dana Della Fave, almost legally changed her name last year just to be eligible."

"Now *that's* crazy," I said after swallowing.

"Her parents didn't go for it," Abby said.

"Shocker," I said dryly.

"What's crazier Jor, is they might give you a bid. Maybe they'll give me a bid too."

"A what now?" I said, deciding my fries could wait.

Abby looked at me like I was the dumbest person she had ever met.

"A bid."

"What's a bid?"

"This girl who's a sophomore was telling me this morning that every year when members of MASCARA graduate, they have to 'rush' new girls to get in. This year, Mara French and Asher Sutherland are graduating. Don't you get it?"

"Not really," I admitted. And I was usually pretty smart.

"They are going to rush new girls that have names that start with the letters 'M' and 'A' to be members!"

In slow motion, what Abby was saying unspooled. That girl, Asher Sutherland, may very well have just asked my real name to see if I could be in her circle. Live some semblance of her life. And for the first time in my life, the name Marjorie may have just taken me somewhere. Somewhere better than Marjorie Car-jorie.

I thought of Dave Doherty and fourth grade. "Marjorie Carjorie she came from the barge-erie. She was a little bit larg-erie. Marjorie Carjorie."

I wasn't even a bit largery. I was tiny then and pretty tiny now. But leave it to grade school to make up something stupid that makes you self-conscious for the rest of your life.

The chanting was faint while Abby boasted on and on about blue make-up and invitations. Her green eyes were greener. Her enthusiasm was, well frightening. If she had a tail it'd be bushy and wiggling.

Don't picture her with a tail, I willed myself.

I tried so hard to give her what she wanted in that moment, but all I could picture was her animated tail. And honestly, why would Asher Sutherland pick us? There were over 300 freshman girls – surely at least ten percent of them had 'M' or 'A' names. Probably thirty something girls and we were so, well, plain. Weren't we?

"You should look up all the girls in our class that start with 'M' and 'A' right away," I said as I finished slurping my soda.

"Oooh, good idea!" Abby said and scooted out of her seat.

"I was kidding," I said under my breath as she walked away.

CHAPTER 2

"I bid you adieu"

The "bid" to join MASCARA was their signature cobalt blue mascara taped to your locker. That's how you know you have been rushed. Which I guess was similar to a sorority. So I've heard anyway. Not the mascara part but you got like a flower or something pretty. In this case, an unopened package of the make-up was how you got invited to at least *try out* to be a MASCARA. The rest of the school semester was basically an audition to maybe do something. Possibly.

MASCARA gave out approximately six bids every year to replace exactly two graduating members. If they need to replace 1 or 3 seniors instead of 2, they adjust the bid quantity.

This year the bids were given to Missy Warwick, Andy Flynn, Megan Welsh, Ashley Walker, Anders Cavelli and myself.

Yes, me Jorie Carr. Who would now be outed to the whole school as Marjorie Carr, and maybe but not certainly, Marjorie Carjorie.

Abby, on the other hand, waited all day for hers to up and appear on her locker. It never did. I saw her do double takes on occasion. When she thought no one was looking, she'd glance at her locker as though she was looking at something else in that direction and dart her eyes over and then shamefully dart them back.

So there I was peeling this once-in-a-lifetime thing from my rusty metal locker door and only a few lockers down was Abby, looking like a puppy whose owner just left it by itself for the first time.

Her face was twisted like a delicious salty pretzel that no one took at the stand at the mall.

I wasn't sure what it all meant. Me getting this bid to potentially change the rest of high school. Abby not getting one at all.

Was I a bad friend if I didn't turn this down?

And did I really want this anyway? A week ago I hadn't even heard of MASCARA and now it was taking over my brain. Literally, I couldn't think about anything else.

I had only spoken to Asher once but for the past week I wanted to wake up and just be her. I had become the captain of her fan club and I had no idea how to deprogram my thinking or un-want this.

I had seen a few of the other girls. It was really incredibly hard not to see them. They had the same Asher way about them. That "love me, love me, everyone else does" way. And they were always in these familial groups that made you feel so left out. Like they had six sisters with them all the time and you were the school's only child.

I bet their parties were so much fun. They probably had them all the time.

Everyone seemed to know who was and wasn't in MASCARA. The boys flocked around their lockers like a pack of birds that someone just threw fresh warm bread to. MASCARA girls barely even noticed the attention anymore. They were numb to it. So focused on other things. I can't imagine boys fawning over me and me just being too preoccupied by the newest shade of nail polish to notice.

I didn't know which girls I had seen. Mara French maybe. She looked like a Mara would. She looked Eastern European with a pale face, light hair and high, defined cheekbones.

I had taken the long way once through the senior hallway that day on purpose. There were a few cute boys that I knew were entirely too old for me but it was fun to window-shop the merchandise. That day I saw the girl with cheekbones so prominent it looked like a sculptor had chiseled her into existence that morning. She also had the fluorescent blue eyelashes framing her ice blue eyes.

She had a Chanel bag. Like, an actual Chanel bag. I didn't know if it was classic Chanel or brand new Chanel because I didn't know these things. Which is exactly why I didn't deserve this bid and shouldn't be in MASCARA. What was I thinking?

I was so stuck on her Chanel in that moment, I barely noticed that the girl holding it had half-smiled at me. Was that at me? I turned, assuming she was smiling at someone behind me. I turned back around just a second too late and bumped smack into some older boy and consequently spilled my notebooks to the floor.

"Look where you're going freshman," he said and laughed. He laughed like a buffoon. I hated buffoon boys.

"Sorry," I muttered.

And that was that. MASCARA girl was gone and I was crouched down in the senior hallway picking up notebooks.

I had seen two more MASCARA girls walking together the following day. One girl made me want to never eat again for the rest of my life. She had light brown perfect skin, faux pieces of red hair feathered into long black locks and the signature blue mascara over blue eyes. She had so many eccentric accessories on, like a line of checkerboard bracelets that almost made a drab uniform look good.

The other girl had a big toothy smile of the whitest teeth I had ever seen. Her makeup was impeccable. Her hair was pulled in a tight bun and she had 1960s-like liner perfectly penned over both eyes. They looked at me, whispered and kept on walking.

I would have to go to the mall and study up on things I didn't know. Like everything.

We had one huge shopping mall in town, Willow Grove. But I always went there with Abby.

And I couldn't very well ask Abby to come with me to Willow Grove that afternoon. I was already smuggling the blue mascara taped on my locker into my book bag like a night bandit so she wouldn't see.

Frankly, I didn't know who to ask. I hardly knew anyone.

Willow Grove Mall was under a mile from my house so I was allowed to go there after school without supervision. I usually rode my bike there on days I wasn't helping at my dad's water and filter shop.

If only I knew more kids at Saint Lawrence. Pretty much everyone I went to middle school with wound up going to Willow Grove High. It was just the way things worked. Like people have breakfast, and then they have lunch. Except of course, for Abby and I, who decided that Saint Lawrence was where we "belonged."

In eighth grade we sat our moms down together and gave them this pitch on why they should basically spend a few thousand dollars a year on their daughters' schooling rather than send them to the perfectly fine and free public school down the street.

Neither of our moms were devout Catholics but they did go to church for good measure on all the days that God was watching. You know, like Easter.

I think it showed some kind of strange initiative for our lives that we wanted, that we were actually begging, to go to private school.

So that's how we wound up in this mess.

"Aren't you going to miss all your friends?" my mom had asked at the time.

"No," I said flatly.

"Besides, I'll have Abby," I added.

My mom knew me better than this. There had to be an ulterior motive – a big, juicy ulterior motive to picking the academy over Willow Grove High School. My ulterior motive played bass guitar and got to school on a skateboard.

As I stuffed the mascara package into my book bag, I noticed there was writing on the back. In blue marker, with heart-dotted "I"'s. Someone *actually* went through the trouble of dotting every "I" with a filled in heart.

Marjorie,

Since that is your real name, we'd like to invite you to rush MASCARA. This tube is yours to keep. If you're interested in finding out more, meet us at Willow Grove at 4 p.m. today. We can explain everything. Meet us at the water fountain downstairs. P.S. Wear the mascara.

Always,
–Asher

Was this real life?

Squatted down, I saw two brown shoes attached to two feet. I knew those shoes.

"Do you want to go to Willow Grove with me today after school?"

It was Abby.

Crap.

I swapped the mascara for my phone and zipped my book bag up, trying hard to make it look like I had been on the ground reading my phone instead of the most amazing package of makeup in the history of ever.

"Did you see I sent you a picture of Missy Warwick's locker? Last period? She got *the* mascara taped to it today. She was bragging to *everyone* in Algebra," Abby said, unaware of my same fortune.

"Really? Bragging?" I asked. I actually gulped. People say they gulp, but they don't really gulp. I took a huge gulp of saliva.

I decided this was neither an admission nor an exclusion of information.

"Nonstop. She was already putting it on in her little mirror-lined compact and fluttering her eyelashes around class," said Abby. "She looked like a deer baby."

"Wow. I didn't see the pic no," I said, knowing damn well what the bids looked like.

"So I was thinking, we should go to the mall and spruce up our wardrobes. It'll make us feel better."

I didn't know what to do here. I couldn't find a way out and I didn't want to tell her yet. I didn't even know how I felt about the whole thing. How would I react if she demanded I didn't join? What if she cried? What if she hated me and then I had literally no one at Saint Lawrence?

I decided maybe I could get her a bid. Maybe if I went today to Willow Grove and talked to the girls and told them how cool Abby was, they'd agree and give one extra bid out tomorrow.

"I can't today but how about tomorrow," I asked, finally.

Abby chewed her lip like she does when she's disappointed. Her braces were always really visible when she did this. I felt bad but it was the only way I could make this right.

"Why, what'dya doing today?"

I felt like a cartoon drawing with a bunch of different thought bubbles above my head that said different things.

Do I tell her?

I'd crush her.

Say something.

Walk away.

I could picture the thought bubbles unbeknownst to Abby just rising to the right and left of my head.

Finally, I snapped out of it and they popped.

"Just homework."

Homework? Really? This was the best I could come up with? It was like the first week of school.

"Suit yourself," Abby said.

Then it dawned on me that she might go anyway. But who would she go with?

"Don't go to Willow Grove today, I'm going home to work on a project. Come with me tomorrow," I said.

"You have projects already?"

"Yes," I said.

This would be the first of many times I lied to Abby.

CHAPTER 3

"Berries Mixed with Crayon"

I can't explain why I was nervous or what I was even nervous about. I had chewed my gum so hard it felt like a soggy rubber band inside my mouth by the time I reached my house.

"How was school?" my mom asked as soon as I walked in.

I didn't want to tell her about MASCARA. Not yet. What if she told Abby's mom? What if she didn't want me to join? I knew if my mom didn't want me to join, I was only going to want to join more. It's just the law of nature or something.

"Fine," I said simply.

What could I possibly say that she would understand anyway? Well Mom, I got invited to change the fate of my next four years of high school and possibly my entire life today? Then I ordered grilled cheese at the cafeteria. You know, no big deal.

"Make any new friends? How's Abby adjusting?" she asked.

God, it was like she had telepathy sometimes.

"Not really. I dunno, good I guess."

My mom gave me a strange look. One that basically said, *Why don't you know how Abby is adjusting? Did you just completely lie to her face just so you could potentially be liked by a group of seven girls you hardly know?*

"I'm going to ride my bike to Willow Grove," was all I said.

I thought about telling her that the best thing she'd ever done was name me Marjorie but then she'd really think I'd finally started experimenting with drugs. My mom knew I hated my name.

"Okay, do you want a ride? I have to pick your brother up from practice in an hour."

"No thanks," I answered, knowing I had to leave now for something I was now lying to everyone about.

I had to get out of there. All of these questions were making me nervous. Plus, I had to change into something a little less "uniform" and a little more "them."

I ran up to my room, threw down my Herschel backpack, and opened my closet. I panned my striped shirts and sweaters, twice. This was no use. I closed the closet. I opened it again. The same way that you open your fridge and there's nothing to eat so you close it but then open it again shortly after, as though some magic elf behind your fridge went to the grocery store and then restocked it while you weren't looking with all new food. What did I really think was going to happen here? A seamstress was busy hiding in the back of my fleeces and stitching me all new clothes? Ridiculous.

I finally figured they had already seen me today and over-trying with my clothes as soon as I got home just for their sake might seem even less cool than my actual wardrobe, so I grabbed an easy pair of jeans and a sweatshirt.

I ran a tortoiseshell comb through my hair in front of my mirror. My mirror had at least twenty pictures of Abby and I stuck to it. My mirror was trying to tell me not to go. Just then I remembered I had to wear the mascara.

I fumbled through my book bag and pulled it out half surprised it was still there. As though it never happened, or it up and ran away on the bus ride home. I peeled the package open gingerly, careful not to rip the back with the writing from Asher. I was actually going to save the note. I'm pathetic.

I once read in a magazine that you aren't actually supposed to pump your mascara brush into the tube, even though people do it all the time. It gets air inside it and dries out the goopy stuff. I didn't really wear make-up. It wasn't that I didn't wear any, but I just didn't like the way it felt on my face sometimes. Like batter. Like a thick layer of something sugary I was going to bake and not what should be on my skin.

I did use a brown eyeliner, actually it was called Chocolate, and I had a lip gloss that I loved called Sunny California. I smeared it on my lips like seven times a day sometimes. It tasted like berries mixed with crayon. Not that I've ever eaten a crayon. Well, I probably did as a kid.

I put the wand to my lashes carefully and tried to steady my hand. One wrong move and I would have electric blue in the whites of my eyes. Every time I applied mascara, which to date was not many, I was afraid I would sneeze and then Choo! and it would be over. Thankfully, I didn't have to sneeze but I imagined this would be horrible.

I watched as my eyes transformed with the outline of indigo cast on them. I didn't think I was the prettiest girl in the world. I mean, I guess I was pretty but in a way that takes someone a while to figure out. Puzzle pretty. As in, no one ever walked in a room and saw me and said, " Oh my God, look at that girl she's so pretty!" but after a while of fitting things together they were more like, "Huh, you're pretty." Like it was a growing shock to them, like I slow cooked in a crock pot for a few hours. But in this moment, with the blue goopy gobby eye paint on, I felt pretty. Really pretty. Walk in the room pretty, not puzzle pretty.

It's weird how odd I felt for thinking that. People aren't supposed to think that they are ugly. But they're not really allowed to think that they are pretty. So was everyone supposed to think of themselves as somewhere in the middle? How silly is that?

I always hear girls saying that they think they are ugly and I think most of the time it's so that someone will correct them and tell them they're pretty. This seems like a lot of extra work to do something you could do yourself.

I finished putting the mascara on and my lashes were so long I felt like I could trip over them. I looked like a Disney princess. I didn't feel like a Disney Princess because I was a little too "Tom-boy" to really feel that way. At least that's what a lot of people called me growing up. "Oh she's such a Tom-boy," they'd say to my Dad. What does "tomboy" even mean? What a stupid word.

Before my brother Matt was born, I guess I did all those boy things that a dad wants a son for although I don't remember any of them. My brother's nine now so it's been a long time since I've tossed a ball or whatever, but to this day I never grew especially girly or Disney princess-y.

Right here, in this moment, I looked a girl. Like I could almost fit in with Asher Sutherland. Okay, maybe that was a stretch. I'd never have hair like her. This was something I would need to admit and accept right now. Her hair was like freshly-rolled silk strands laid gently on her head every morning by a golden gnome, that never kinked or split or most of all bloated out by humidity and gave in to frizz. The more I thought about her, ugh, the more I hated her. In the "switch your life with me" kind of way.

Okay. So that's it. I've decided that I'm going. I've put the mascara on. I'm obviously going to go through with this. It's too late to turn back.

I had heard my polka dotted phone vibrate now at least three times but I refused to look at it. I needed to focus. I took one last glance in the mirror before I accidentally saw the clock and realized I was going to be late – and something told me it was not considered fashionable in this case.

I ran down the stairs so fast it sounded like a herd of elephants. I didn't want my mom to see my eyelashes or the questions would start. I would have thrown on sunglasses but then she'd be even more suspicious and think I was doing drugs.

"Okay bye!" I threw out causally into the air hoping she'd hear me.

"Do you need any money Jor?" my mom called to me from the living room.

"Nah I'm okay. I get my paycheck Saturday and have enough on me for a shirt or something," I said quickly.

Denying money was a definite red flag to my mom. Why would I say no to money before a trip to the mall?

Hurry, hurry, I commanded myself.

I practically scaled the walls to get to my garage and then behaved like I was robbing my own bike. I threw my leg over the seat and half-hopped on. Thankfully, the garage was open so I didn't waste any time tampering with buttons.

As soon as I was out front, I glanced back to make sure my mother's tiny head wasn't perched in some window somewhere.

With that, I began peddling as quickly as I could to Willow Grove. I thought about this pinky swear that Abby and I had made over the summer to not drift apart in high school. I peddled faster. What was a pinky swear anyway? Why did people swear on a specific finger? Was I breaking the promise to her already?

I could feel the beginning of autumn in the air as I peddled on. That unmistakable smell and that cool crispness of leaves even when they haven't yet turned or fallen. It was here. And pretty soon winter would be too. I kept peddling. I started picturing a judge asking me on a stand if I had pinky sworn to tell the whole truth.

Pedal, pedal. Faster, faster.

Finally, I reached the main entrance of Willow Grove.

The masculine glass door was centered between a Black and White Boutique and a Gibson's Leathers. I locked my bike up as fast as my hands would allow, knowing it was already 4 o'clock.

As soon as the lock CHIT-CLICKED into place, I was darting for the food court where the water fountain was. I imagined that to the passerby shoppers in the mall I looked half insane run-walking as fast I could but still trying to look composed and chasing my breath in most places. Plus I had tons of blue mascara on my eyes.

I stopped, momentarily, to let my breath catch up to me in front of a frozen yogurt kiosk. I inhaled a few times while I watched a woman and man literally collect their yogurt stream together. Like they both needed to touch the cup while the soft pile spilled in circular motions along the inside. I may be young, and maybe I've never really been in "love" love, but this was just overdramatic.

I did my best not to roll my eyes and kept on for the fountain. Calmer now, after mentally laughing at the soap opera couple from FroYoLow, I marched over to the backwards heads of girls with perfect hair and perpendicular plaids. All still in uniform. All nodding in uniform. Bleagh.

I recognized Anders Cavelli from my homeroom. I imagined the other three girls on the edge of the fountain that sat kind of conjoined; Missy Warwick, Ashley Walker and Megan Welsh were all probably in homeroom together too because of their last names. Which only left Andy Flynn who was likely the girl more or less alone. I sized them all up.

One girl was standing and speaking to the seated cluster of five girls on the fountain's edge. I joined the seated cluster and shut up, careful not to snicker at the yogurt couple. Careful not to worry about Abby. Careful not to think of the many, many wishes beneath me in the fountain attached to tossed pennies. Careful, to listen to who I could only assume, was Mara French. It was the girl I saw in the senior hallway that day.

"Next, is that we don't use acronyms. Ever. There will be no 'LOL' this or 'LMFAO' that. It's stupid and frankly, MASCARA is the only acronym that you need to know," the girl (probably Mara) said with confidence.

"Got it?" she asked the group.

I looked to my left and watched as a row of heads nodded in zombaic unison. Zombaic isn't a word but if it was, it would perfectly describe the brainwashed thing that I saw happening before me.

Don't picture Zombies. Don't picture zombie videos. Don't picture a zombie apocalypse.

As I pried my brain away from Zombie images, I got my thoughts caught back on the sunken wishes and there I stayed in my head until Mara asked me a question I wasn't even listening to.

"Do you need us to repeat the first few rules since you are late, freshman?" apparently she asked.

I say apparently, because then, out of nowhere she said, "I *said*, do you need us to repeat the first few rules since you are late, freshman?"

This lead me to believe that she had already asked this once and I was stupidly gazing at the coins underwater drumming up all the things that people in this town could possibly wish for before hurling them in.

This was a rookie move. This was a move for a freshman.

I felt my cheeks getting hotter and my throat sort of did this half-closing thing it does sometimes when I think about swallowing. In seconds I'd be sweating if I didn't say something. Why did I wear a sweatshirt? All the other girls that were rushing stayed in uniform.

"I'm so sorry, I just think coins in fountains are..." I started, and then began to struggle because honestly what did I think coins in fountains are and then I remembered that corny couple and suddenly out came... "romantic!"

I watched as Asher, who was seated ever-so-coolly and nonchalantly behind Mara (or girl-I-think-is-Mara), shot her huge eyes over at her and said, "I love that!"

Girl-I-think-is-Mara turned around like she'd been hit with a crossbow arrow. "You do?" she asked, somewhat disgusted.

"What's not to love?" Asher asked and stood up. I noticed her nails were painted plaid, like Burberry came over this morning and did them for her. She placed her hands in the back pocket of her corduroy pants.

"Marjorie right?" she asked.

Ugh. What was I going to do now?

"Yes," I said.

"Since I love what you just said, I'm going to repeat what you missed quickly for you," Asher said. "We can always fill you in on details later."

This was crazy. This whole scene was crazy. A handful of jaw-dropped freshman looked at me like I was crazy and frankly, I felt crazy because Asher Sutherland was doing me this, like, public favor because I said some amazing thing. I couldn't even remember what I said in that moment but I wanted to say it every day because I felt like I had power for the very first time in my whole little life.

"Rule one is you must hold a chair position in MASCARA. It's non-negotiable. There are seven chair positions, like Social Chair, or Contact Chair – and a suitable one will be assigned to you," Asher said.

Mara looked like someone stole her lunch. "I can repeat them," she said.

Mara took this tiny little (but noticeable) step in front of Asher and started ruling the meeting. "Rule two is that you must be logged into the MASCARA app at all times. Yes, there's an app. Asher's Dad literally made it. No joke."

Asher just nodded her head.

After that there were rules that followed that made sense, like getting above a "B" average in school. Then there were the ones that were flat out ridiculous...

"No popping pimples, under any circumstances," Mara said.

I laughed a little thinking she was joking. She wasn't.

"So what do you do?" I asked earnestly.

"Toothpaste," Asher answered, matter-of-factly.

The other girls on the fountain ledge had obviously already heard this strange anecdotal part of the rules so I decided not to act shocked.

"Toothpaste," I said without asking.

"Toothpaste," Asher confirmed with a hard smile.

"Oh, and we always sign off with 'always'."

"Huh?" just sort of left my mouth.

"When we leave a MASCARA, sign a card, text, what have you. It's not 'bye' or 'tootles' or 'love ya' or whatever. You always say 'always' because that's what MASCARA is there for. Always."

I did this weird half nod that I knew only felt cool but didn't look cool and waited for the rest of the rules, the new ones that no one had heard yet. The girls on the ledge perked up around me. They straightened their spines and smoothed over pleats and re-crossed their legs. They planted their chins in their palms and their elbows on their knees and just awaited instruction.

There was so much zombaic culture brewing. One girl even took notes. Like in a notebook. Another made notes in her phone.

I poked the girl next to me, pretty sharply.

"Ow what?" she blurted, annoyed.

"Is that Mara French?" I whispered.

"If you don't know that that's Mara French why are you even here?" the girl barked at me, in a low tone. She had a point. This was the girl I assumed was Andy Flynn. Who I semi-felt bad for when I first walked up the fountain because she didn't have any homeroom friends.

Andy Flynn, I no longer feel bad for you, I mentally noted.

"I don't know," I whisper-hissed back. She looked a little afraid of me and I decided that was okay.

Mara (who I now know for sure is Mara) continued administering the rules.

"No directly telling anyone that you're rushing MASCARA, let them figure it out" and "no boyfriends during the pledge period" and "you must wear the mascara everyday" and "no leaving MASCARA until graduation" and "never talk bad about a MASCARA," were the ones I remembered.

I honed in on two MASCARA girls that were behind Asher, who was still behind Mara. They were looking at each other's phones and swiping screens through like a million apps and laughing and in general, having the best time I'd ever seen two people have. I wanted their life. Was that weird?

I didn't care.

One sat Indian-style with a stack of fashion magazines in her lap and bright yellow ear buds crawling up into her ears. She was one of the girls I had seen last week. She had mocha skin like she'd been massaged with java beans. Her hair came down in long jet black waves with a few pieces of pinkish-red mixed in. She had blue eyes like a Siamese cat and wore a baggy coat that her frail arms got lost in.

On her quick and nimble hands were a tar-colored manicure that probably this girl and only this girl could pull off and of course, blue coated her lashes. I thought I saw a Henna tattoo on her hand. Her clothes were the most original I had ever seen. She had layered knee high socks, not one pair but three stacked to build stripes beneath her kneecaps in contrasting patterns, a fitted skirt with huge buttons, heels I couldn't walk in if I tried, and a sweater that just sort of fell on her. She looked like she just walked out of a magazine.

The girl that she sat and joked with was equally intimidating. She was the only full-on brunette (I forget if I told you I'm a brunette) I had seen thus far in MASCARA and looked so pedigreed she could have entered Westminster, without a dog, and still win. Her thighs were thin (so thin) and hugged by thigh high European (I think) leather boots. She looked like she rode horses. She looked like owned horses. She probably nursed baby horses in her spare time.

I was finding it harder and harder to pay attention. There were a ton of rules all blending together. I still didn't understand the rush process but I was really starting to want it. All of it.

Two more MASCARA girls walked up to join the group. I hadn't seen them before. They looked closer to my age.

Mara finally wrapped up the endless rules with "Every MASCARA must never leave the house in sweats" which was borderline ridiculous. I mean, we weren't going to wind up in some *STARS, THEY'RE JUST LIKE US* headline in a gossip magazine. So many rules.

I was never good at following rules. Abby was good at following rules. She was so much more suited for this than I was. And then I remembered my plan.

I half-raised my hand. Are we supposed to raise our hands to talk here?

"Freshman?" Mara urged.

"Do people get bids after today? I mean, um, how likely is it to give out another bid, for, for this year?"

Mara gave a slight laugh and then glanced backwards at Asher.

"How likely are we Asher?"

The two girls in the back giggled. It sounded like one said "one hundred percent unlikely" but maybe I was hearing things.

Asher finally stepped in.

"We don't give out any bids, under any circumstances, after today. I know it seems like you were randomly selected but I assure you that isn't the case. It's formulaic to a fault. Every one of you was carefully picked by one of us. The only MASCARA member who didn't put a bid out was Carmen, behind me, because she has a sister in your grade and it precludes her from unbiased choosing. Carmen, can you explain that part," Asher said and gestured with her how-does-she-have-the-time-to-wait-for-a-manicure-like-that hand.

The dark skinned girl put down her doodads and magazines and disconnected from her tangled wire of earbuds to join Asher.

She spoke.

"My sister, Mercedes Banks, is in your class. So basically, I can't vote this year. Someone else could have picked her but they didn't," she said shooting a telling look at super-pedigreed girl who was starting to resemble Princess Kate.

Mercedes Banks, I thought. *Could she have a name that sounded richer?*

"Okay Carmen, that's enough," Asher said and continued. "On the back of each of your mascara bids, someone wrote you an invitation to come here today. Each one of them is different. That'll tell you who voted you in. But to answer your question, it's a simple no. No more bids will be given out."

I felt panicked. Not only did I lie to Abby but now it was all for nothing. I couldn't get her a bid plain and simple. And what's worse was that I had to wear the mascara to school tomorrow, so before first period she'd know everything. I fidgeted in my non-seat on the fountain and started to play out how this would go with Abby tomorrow. It was gruesome in my head.

Then Asher broke my thoughts and it occurred to me that she was the one who "chose" me. There was no way I could bail now. I mean this girl was the most popular senior in school and she chose me. Me. Puzzle pretty me with bad penmanship and a part time job at a water store. My parents' water store. I sold water. Something that is free. How much less MASCARA-like could I be?

"Okay girls, so just a few more things that you need to know about the actual process. As most of you know, I'm Asher Sutherland, this is Mara French next to me. We're both graduating at the end of the year. So obviously, we need to replace an "M' and an "A" which is why you guys are here," Asher explained.

I usually walked away in my head while people talked and instead daydreamed about nonsense but I was glued to her *every* word.

"The rush, or some call it 'pledge' or 'recruitment' process, for MASCARA is all first semester or until you are down to two, whichever comes first. Obviously only two of you will get in by winter break, but you'll only be a MASCARA-in-waiting, because we haven't yet graduated. You'll learn more about that later. In the mean time, some of you will drop out because you just can't hack it and if none of you do, we have no choice but to blackball four of you by then. We don't want to but we have to."

I felt a knot in my stomach. Blackball? That sounded humiliating.

Asher continued. "Other things you need to know right now: As you heard, we have an app. My dad built it four years ago and it's just for us. It's password protected and none of you will get the password until you are in. As you also have heard, we all have chair positions. Some more examples are Fashion Chair, which Carmen holds," she said and pointed with her body toward Carmen. "There's a beauty chair which Rachel Whitley – behind me here – holds and Music Chair which Mara holds. This is to always keep us in front of everything that's trending."

Out of the far corner of my eye, I saw the other girls I was now rushing with or pledging with or whatever hanging on Asher's every word. There wasn't a chance in Hell any of them were going to drop out. They looked like Asher addicts. I really wasn't one to talk. I felt secretly invincible that she picked me.

Don't picture a superhero cape.

"You're going to find out instructions as you go and you'll be given weekly tasks. The tasks will get harder as the weeks go by. It's designed that way to see who really wants it. Pay attention to your lockers, you'll be getting notes often from whomever picked you. They are more or less there to guide you. Any questions?"

I did have a question. Well, truthfully, I had a hundred questions. Like how you break the news to your best friend who didn't get a bid even though she should have.

Anders Cavelli piped up. "What would happen if there weren't the right first letters of first names? Like, not enough "M"'s and "A"'s this year?" she asked.

It was actually a good question. I didn't want to nod or anything in case "they" thought it was a dumb question.

"It rarely happens but if it does, the seven active members can move to create a whole new name for the incoming freshman class and beyond. It requires a 'yes' vote by every member though," Asher said to the group.

"Ten years ago we were actually called LASHES. They couldn't find anyone qualified with an "H" name after only two years, rumor has it," Mara added. "Turns out, the letters in 'mascara' are actually pretty easy to find."

"Yes, very feminine," Carmen said from behind Mara.

Anders just sort of nodded and shut up. She may have been blushing.

With that, Asher took back the conversation. "Last thing I want to do is let you girls know who all of us are and give you contact sheets. DO NOT give out our numbers to anyone. Not even for emergencies."

Another girl I hadn't yet seen began handing out the contact sheets. The sheets of paper were, not surprisingly, cobalt blue.

"Okay so you all know Mara French and myself. You've also met Carmen Banks, please do not let her sister know we were chatting about her. Over there is Rachel Whitley whom I have mentioned. Rachel and Carmen are juniors at Saint Lawrence. And last but not least are our sophomores. Amanda Betancourt is handing you your contact sheets. Amanda is, appropriately, Contact Chair. Smile Amanda," Asher said.

With that the girl handing out the blue sheets smiled, unveiling two deep dimples. She was just plain symmetrically gorgeous. She had high hair like a pop singer that I loved and big pouty lips.

Asher continued, "Sue Cameron isn't here because she is at cheer-leading practice and will be ninety-nine percent of the time you need her. She's the bounciest blond in the pyramid. Sue is Community Chair. Finally, Adrianna Mackey, who we call 'Macs' is M.I.A., which is common for Macs. Her brothers are also the hottest guys in school but Rob is

Mara's boyfriend and so therefore he's off the market. Derek Mackey is single though," Asher trailed off. I thought I heard a slight squeal.

Note to self...learn how to act girlier and squeal.

"Yes well, that wraps it up!" Mara piped in. "You're free to go. Instructions to come by homeroom tomorrow."

She turned to Asher. "Must you always tell them about Robbie?"

My head was spinning. I wanted to go home and draw a chart so I keep all of the girls straight. I wish I had seen what Sue and Adrianna looked like.

As long as I knew who the seniors were. What was it about older kids that made them so important anyway? I didn't get it but Asher and Mara were like Gods just because they were seniors. Well that, and because they were flawless.

CHAPTER 4

"Carmen Banks"

I decided to troll the mall for just a little while before leaving. I was playing Carmen's outfit over in my mind trying to think, what would Carmen buy? Like a WWCB bumper sticker. I mean, she had so many clinky, clangy fun things on. The girl clanked. She literally made jangly noises when she moved from her buckles and rings and belts and things I wouldn't have a clue how to pick out. I needed help. I needed a Fashion Chair.

I needed to scream at the top of my lungs in this mall because my brain was on fast-forward and I unfortunately but fortunately got picked for this club that I so unfortunately fortunately wanted to be in.

AAAAAAHHHHHHH, I thought, loudly. It's weird to think a loud thought. I mean, thoughts have no volume but that thought was loud and screamy. How? It can't be any louder than any other no volume thought.

As I thought about thoughts, and ran my hand down the arm of a shirt I really, really liked and was juuuuust about to reach for the price tag I couldn't afford, a hand was on my shoulder.

I broke my thought thoughts and twirled around to find Abby looking confused and maybe angry.

No, definitely angry.

"I thought you were staying in to do a project," said Abby, hand on hip. "And why are you wearing blue mascara? I think it's like code that you can't unless you're pledge—"

I watched the "Oh I get it" moment happen in Abby's brain. It wasn't my favorite moment. It was precisely *the* moment where Abby realized she hated me and I realized that there was no fixing this for the rest of our high school lives.

The very, very worst part?

That I couldn't think of an alternative to pledging MASCARA.

As in, it wasn't even an option for me to offer to *not* do it, for her or for anyone. It was as though the entire group had a hold on me now; the cult hold I made fun of earlier chanted its way into my brain and now held me hostage.

I pictured the inside circle of MASCARA girls and how cozy and utterly inviting their whole lives looked today and then I pictured high school without them.

Days of sitting with Abby and listening to her on repeat that they didn't give her a bid but should have and me meeting Asher's big eyes across the cafeteria as she shook her perfect head of hair in disappointment. The other girls would cock their heads back and laugh at how foolish I was.

"They gave you a bid? They gave you a bid and you didn't tell me?"

Oh boy.

This was bad. This was really, especially bad. I didn't take my hand off the shirtsleeve. I was frozen. And, I really wanted that shirt.

Why was I thinking of a shirt at a time like this?

"Abby, it wasn't like that. I wanted to see if I could get you a bid, that's why I came. That way, if I did, I could surprise you with it."

"And did you?"

I gulped. This time, a sour tasting gulp. Now what?

"I'm working on it," I lied. Lie number two. Who was I? Why was I quickly becoming the worst best friend in the history of best friends?

I pictured a long aged scroll of best friends since 1818 unraveling and there I was at the bottom with a big red circle around my face. WORST BEST FRIEND branded over my name.

Abby stood there. Waiting. Like I didn't hear what she said. I knew that look. Everyone gave me it.

"What?"

"They said 'no' didn't they? They don't give bids after recruitment day. Everyone knows that," she said.

Why does everyone know everything about MASCARA except me?

"When they find out how cool you are, they will change their minds. How could they not? They just need to be told about you."

I sort of meant this. It was a half-truth. Abby was cool, no ifs, ands or buts about it. Would MASCARA give her a bid? Not a chance.

Abby looked the least bit hopeful. Like a puppy waiting for a treat.

"Okay, please try. I know you'd never do it without me and I don't want to hold you back," Abby said.

I heard the loud screeching of brakes in my head. Did she just say what I think she just said? That I'd never do it without her? This wasn't good.

I pulled the shirt off the hanger and draped it on my arm. Then I touched Abby's arm in a Momly way.

"Let me talk to Asher and make certain she knows you're amazing," I comforted.

"What are you on first name basis with Asher Sutherland now?"

Abby laughed as she said it, like it was impossible.

I shrugged. Was I? I didn't really know if I was or wasn't. She did pick me herself though. I wasn't going to tell Abby that. Why add insult to injury?

I stayed quiet.

"Well, I'm headed home. I probably won't come to the mall tomorrow but I'll see you in school," she said.

She was mad.

I knew she was mad, but somehow, now I kind of felt angry too. I mean, I would have never stopped her from rushing MASCARA if she got picked and I didn't. I would have been happy for her. Wouldn't I have?

"Okay," was all I said.

I grabbed a scarf and a belt before making it to the checkout line. I didn't know if I'd ever wear them. They weren't me. They were outspoken. Hell, they were yelling.

As I stood in line, a voice came from over my shoulder.

"This belt is definitely better. It says bad ass and yours says trying to be bad ass," the voice said.

I turned around, and as though my penny in the fountain wish had been granted, there was Carmen Banks giving me fashion advice. Too good to be true. She had an armful of clothes and accessories in her arm. I just *knew* she shopped here. *Sigh* was where all the popular kids always got their clothes, no matter what school they went to. It was a little more money than I liked to spend though so I usually avoided it. Hence, *sigh*.

I took the belt she extended and put mine down on a nearby shelf knowing fair well I would never be caught dead in it now.

"Thanks, I appreciate that," I said earnestly.

"Just another word of advice?"

"Of course, please. Is it the shirt? Too plain?" I asked.

"No, the shirt is cute, buy it. Ditch the freshman cling-on friend though."

Carmen didn't even look up when she said it, just rifled through the hangers on her forearm.

'What do you mean?" I asked, fearing what she was about to say.

She said it anyway. "That girl. The one who was just giving you the third degree in here. Bad news. Get rid of her."

She held a pair of pants to her waist and surveyed a wall mirror.

"Oh she wasn't gi-, she just," I stuttered.

The cashier waved me on. "Next in line, step up please," the cashier said, with no idea what she was interrupting.

"I'm just trying to help you out," Carmen said, still admiring the pants in hand.

I fumbled to get my things on the counter, clearly nervous. I wanted to defend Abby, I really did but this was hardly the right setting. Plus, I was a little upset with her at the moment.

"If you don't, they'll more than likely make you," Carmen added. "Just a word of advice"

"Sixty-three fifty," the cashier prompted.

Ugh. I couldn't concentrate. I blindly felt in my bag for my wallet, all the while my brain was trying to process. Sadly, one of the biggest things that mattered to me right in that moment was that I had an ugly "kid" wallet that I didn't want Carmen to see.

I was sure her wallet would be designer and slender and leather and so adult looking and mine was this scrappy looking denim thing with loose threads popping out of a rainbow. How did I never replace this? That should have been at the top of my list before starting high school, for Christ's sake.

"You know what? You can go ahead of me, I think I want to grab something else," I said to Carmen as I turned from the cashier.

The cashier looked just slightly annoyed. "Would you mind just holding this for me for a just a sec, I'll be right back," I said to her.

I watched Carmen unload all kinds of amazingness. Studded this and herringbone that. A bracelet that sort of looked like a weapon instead of a bracelet. A cargo jacket and a lace skirt. How did she think of these things? I should ask her. No I shouldn't.

As I slowly maneuvered my way back through the circular racks, I spotted a wallet on the clearance rack. Maybe today was my lucky day. It wasn't high fashion but it was both adult and bold (yellow, not ugly yellow but cute yellow) and I had a feeling it was MASCARA-approved.

I still wanted Carmen to leave the store before I went back to the cashier. My best friend basically walked away angry at me ten minutes ago and my biggest focus was not showing a girl I have known for three seconds my childish rainbow wallet. Seriously, who was I becoming?

"Bye Jorie, remember what I said!" Carmen yelled from across the store and waved. "Oh, and I love that yellow wallet you're holding!"

Score.

"Bye Carmen! Thank you!"

CHAPTER 5

"The (pronounced with a long 'e' like 'theeee') guy"

The first time I saw him, I knew right in that moment that I would never forget it as long as I lived. I was standing at my locker wearing most of my new stuff but trying hard to look like I didn't just buy it all yesterday. It was the day after the mall debacle that made Abby hate me. It was also the day after Carmen told me that I basically had to de-friend my best friend – which was never going to happen.

I had the blue mascara on my eyelashes and more people had stared at me before first period than they had all month. I shared the glory in homeroom since Anders Cavelli was also in my homeroom and also wore hers. She didn't say a word to me and I didn't say a word to her.

I was fumbling with a small blue envelope that was clearly slipped through the grates of my locker when I heard two words. That was it. Two words that I had heard before, whether they were broken up into single words or even as a pair.

"Hey, congrats."

That was it.

A commonplace phrase made to sound like it was the first time the words had ever been strung together. I heard "Hey, congrats," somewhere faintly over my right shoulder as someone still moving said them. I turned and saw Derek Mackey for the very first time, walking, no, strutting, toward the senior hallway. Even his walk was interesting. The brother of Adrianna Mackey and I was fairly certain, he was made up entirely of magnets.

His polo shirt was messily tucked into his grey slacks with the back corner popping loose. He had a bag draped over his shoulder instead of piggy-backing his back. He wore a few trendy rings on his narrow fingers and a black slender leather band around his wrist. His hair looked like he just woke up and his smile, his smile went on for days. He was toxic. Good toxic and bad toxic all rolled into one human and in that moment I wanted nothing shy of toxicity. I felt drunk and very, very sobered all at the same time.

"Thanks," I called. It sounded like a question not an answer.

I knew in that second that even the way this boy wore a t-shirt was poisonous. He walked alone, no friends in sight and glanced half-heartedly at me to meet my stare. His smile was crooked but infectious. And then he was gone.

It was seconds, maybe minutes, before I caught my breath. I heard the CLANG of a locker door shut and came to. Abby was staring at me. Staring at my now blue lashes and new clothes and now drooling over my new crush... She was possibly waiting for me to say something.

I turned to look at her. I felt instantly awful. I also felt like I was going to pass out.

"Abby," I started.

"What, now you're going to pine over Derek Mackey? How very cliché," she said. She was filled with venom. Who was this girl?

"I-," I trailed off.

Abby began to walk away.

"Abby wait," I said.

I'd all but forgotten about the blue note in my locker and just about everything else I was doing. I couldn't even think about school or the fact that I had less than a minute before the bell rang for first period.

"I'm gonna be late," Abby said.

With that, she hoofed off to her class and I stood in the hallway. Completely alone.

I couldn't even remember where my class was. Or that my birthday was next week. Or what my name was. As I slowly started walking, the jangly noises of my new Carmen-approved belt reminded me that I was forgetting the card I had pulled from my locker and the fact that despite my best efforts, I very much looked forward to what was inside.

Marjorie-

Congrats on getting a bid for MASCARA. I have nothing but confidence in you. Next week, there's a day called Senior Slave Day. It falls on the school's Dress Down Day. But before that, I'd like to invite you to sleep over my house this weekend – get you prepped. There is so much to go over and I have to give you your first pledge task. Don't worry, this one is easy, as long as you have the drive.

Always,
- Asher

The bell rang. I was late. I had barely been a student here for a week and a half and I was already late. Wonderful.

I tucked the note away and started for first period, trying so hard to wipe Derek Mackey from my head.

"I love that belt," a girl I didn't know said to me in passing.

"Oh, thanks," I said sheepishly.

Where was my classroom? I opened a notebook where I had a copy of my schedule (it was also in my phone and taped to the inside of my locker) and saw 102 next to first period. I had to start memorizing this thing.

As I rounded the mustard-colored hallway for room 102, I saw Mara French and who I could only guess was Rob Mackey (he looked a little like Derek) making out against a wall. They were right next to my door. Really?

"Excuse me," I said quietly.

The two unlocked lips.

"Oh Robbie, this is Marjorie, our new pledgling," Mara said.

I felt paralyzed. Like my arms were stuck to my sides and my book bag weighed 400 pounds. Like I was an amputee and my arms had been cut off at my shoulders by my book bag straps. I stood there for a good, long second.

"Hey," was all I got out. I felt my face heat.

"Hey little MASCARA-in-training," the boy laughed.

"Don't call her that," Mara said, sternly.

"Oh stop," he said to her. He looked at me. "You coming to the party next weekend?"

"No," I said.

"Well why the hell not?" he asked.

"Oh, they'll be there," Mara said to him. She barely looked at me.

"Sweet, Macs parties are the best in school, you know," he said to me like he was teaching me something.

"I have to get to class. It was nice meeting you," I said and scooted by.

I slowly pulled the very closed door to my class that was very much in progress open. Everyone looked. Ugh, I hated that so very much.

Sometimes, if you're lucky, you have teachers who just keep right on teaching when you're "that person" who interrupts class in session. This way, you can hang your head in shame, beeline for your desk and awkwardly assemble your things.

Not this class.

"Ms. Carr, thank you for joining us," Mr. Walsh said. The whole class looked.

I wanted to bury my head into something. I saw a few of the kids start whispering and I knew, wholeheartedly, that it was about my blue makeup choice.

I walked swiftly to the only available desk in the room and slid in.

As I clumsily tried to set my books on the teeny tiny table that the desk offered, I heard, "She got a bid."

I turned behind me and saw a girl I didn't know whispering to a boy I didn't know. Both were staring at me and not even bothering to try to look like they weren't.

What was I going to do here? I had the Scarlett letter lashes looming over my eyelids. It was no use. I turned back and began scribbling on a notebook and pretended I was taking notes.

My mind quickly wandered to Derek Mackey. Mara had said we would be there at some party I was only now hearing about, assumedly, at his house. This got better (or worse) by the second.

Suddenly, I could care less about being late, making my teacher upset (new for me), the people talking behind my back or my own best friend. What was going on?

I scribbled my name across an empty page over and over again. Jorie Carr. Jorie Carr. I even wrote Marjorie once and quickly crossed it out.

Mr. Walsh lectured about the Battle of Bunker Hill. How I wished I liked history.

I felt like more and more pairs of eyes were landing on me, examining me, like this was biology class.

I briefly pictured myself in the Battle of Bunker Hill, taking them all out one by one. My mind drifted.

Try as I may, I couldn't get that simple "hey, congrats" out of my head. Or sleeping over at Asher's. And what was Senior Slave Day? Now a party. A "Macs" party as Rob put it. It sounded so very juvenile but I wanted nothing more in life at this moment than to be part of their slang. To call them "Macs." I wanted to see Adrianna, who I still didn't even know for sure what she looked like, and say "What's up Macs" and this whole line of thinking was ridiculous. All of it. Concentrate, Bunker Hill.

BANG.

The worst thought finally reared its ugly head. Was I going to be allowed to go to these things? I had only ever really slept out at Abby's house. My mom was going to freak when she found out Abby wasn't going to any of these things.

Damn it, Bunker Hill....

Bunker. Hill.

Nod.

Mr. Walsh's eyes were on me, I just knew they were. He could tell my brain was somewhere else entirely.

Concentrate Jorie.

I looked down at my notebook which now had my name branded all over it like a cheap ad for Jorie Carr fragrances or something.

1775. Revolutionary War. Blah blah blah.

Suddenly, without warning, the bell rang. How was that even possible? I had spent an entire class period spinning myself into a MASCARA-inspired tornado of nothing important at all.

I ejected myself from my desk seat. Since my room was adjacent to the junior hallway, I thought if I got out early enough I might just catch a glimpse of Derek Mackey. Why did I want to see him so badly? Was he even a junior? He had to be if Adrianna was a sophomore and Rob was a senior. There were no Mackey twins, right? Perish the thought.

I hustled toward the door and someone tapped my shoulder.

"Jorie, right?" a boy I had never seen before asked.

"Sure," I said, distracted.

"I was wondering if you had already made plans for the Halloween Dance," he muttered.

"The what?"

"The Halloween dance, next month?" he asked.

I scrambled my brain to come up with something, anything. It was mid-September. What was he talking about?

"I haven't," I said.

"Well, maybe we can go together. That is, if you don't have plans," the boy said.

"Maybe," I said and half-smiled. "I'll, um get back to you."

He was even kind of cute but my mind was elsewhere.

As I maneuvered past him, a girl with a face drowning in freckles ambushed the conversation.

"Are you really pledging MASCARA?" she asked.

Think Marjorie, think. What was I supposed to say here? I couldn't remember.

Don't tell anyone directly, let them figure it out.

"Uh, maybe," I said, half-asking.

"Oh my God, that is so cool. Are you going to, like, all their parties?" the girl continued.

Was I? I had no idea. Suddenly, things were moving very fast and I didn't know what to say to anyone.

I walked side-by-side through the door with the over-inquisitive girl, who I didn't know by name, when I saw a semi-familiar face. The toothy, could-be-an ad-for-Colgate girl with the tight bun caught my gaze and walked over.

"Marjorie," she said.

I nearly pulled a "Who, me?" but then I realized this was my ticket out of the uncomfortable conversation I was stuck in.

"Yeah," I confirmed.

The perfect smile girl gave a look to the freckle girl asking my life story and with that, freckle girl got bashful and walked off.

"You looked like you could be saved. I'm Adrianna," the girl said, her smile blinding. "Mackey."

"Oh right, thank you," I said.

"My brother Derek said you were cute," Adrianna said. "You totally are adorable."

Suddenly, the entire school stopped. Or at least it felt like it did. Did I just hear her right?

"I—," I stammered. I actually stammered.

I felt my cheeks fill with color.

"Don't let it go to your head," she said with a comforting laugh.

"Oh, of course, no," I said.

"Are you sleeping at Asher's this weekend?" she asked.

I couldn't even tell someone how to tie a shoelace right now. It was too much. This whole thing was just too much. Still, I couldn't sound stupid.

"I think I am," I said.

"Awesome," Adrianna said. "Good luck on your first task."

I didn't even know if I was walking anymore. I was quite possibly floating but still really needed to come up for air.

We reached the end of the junior hallway and then, at the end of the row of lockers, I saw him, leaning, and talking to another boy.

He had the longest eyelashes I had ever seen on a boy. He was grinning wide and looking directly at me and his sister. I had to get out of this.

"Derek!" Adrianna called and waved.

"Okay well thanks, I'll see ya around," I said quickly.

"Blue looks great on you," Adrianna said to me.

I met his eyes, just for a second, before taking off. Almond shaped and heavy. I wanted to talk to him so badly but I couldn't. Not yet. I was reeling from this day and needed a breather.

Plus, I couldn't be late to another class.

I waltzed back into the freshman hallway and saw Abby standing at the locker of a girl I didn't know.

This made me, very irrationally, upset.

I stopped and triangled myself in as non-awkwardly as I could.

"Hey, sorry to interrupt," I said.

The girl that Abby was talking to, before I so rudely interrupted, stared at my eyes. I was growing tired of everyone judging me before I even spoke.

"Abby, I was wondering if you changed your mind about the mall today," I said.

Abby looked at the floor.

"I'm actually going to go with Sara," she said.

"Who's Sa—," I started.

"I'm Sara, it's nice to meet you," the girl said, still staring at my eyelashes.

I didn't know what to say. Or do.

I suddenly felt like I was being cheated on.

"Okay, see you guys later," I said.

"Okay," Abby said, without looking at me. "See ya."

I had to book it to second period if I was going to be on time. What was happening here? I walked swiftly through the hallway to my next class. I saw Amanda Betancourt and a blond I assumed was Sue Cameron walk the other way, their arms were linked. The blond looked like a cheerleader. She had to be Sue. Amanda noticed me breeze by but didn't say anything.

Right before I walked into my class, I saw a flier hanging by a corner for the Halloween Dance.

Why would this boy ask me to go when he didn't even know me, weeks in advance?

I walked into the classroom just making it on time and rushed toward the back of the room. There were only a few open seats left as far as I could tell.

Again, I felt like everyone was staring at me. I was becoming truly paranoid.

"Nice lashes," a girl I had never seen before said as I walked past.

I couldn't tell if she was being mean or complementing me.

Seriously? This was Religion class. Shouldn't people care about more important things? Like Jesus?

I took a seat.

I positioned my book bag so that I could quickly glance at my phone before the teacher noticed. I had heard Mrs. Davenport was a stickler when it came to using phones in class. She had already confiscated two in the last week and I wasn't about to get mine taken. Not now.

I noticed a text message on my home screen from a number with no name:

Hey Jorie, it's Asher. I need to talk to you about Derek Mackey. Meet me in the senior hallway at the end of the day. I'll give you a ride home.

CHAPTER 6

"First and Last Name Guys"

Word sure traveled fast around Saint Lawrence. I mean, what was there to talk about regarding Derek Mackey and me? I wasn't sure that I cared what there was to talk about if I was getting to ride home, publicly in front of everyone, with Asher Sutherland. I hadn't even seen the parking lot yet.

All freshman ever got to do was walk from the smelly buses straight into school and at the end of the day, pile right back on. It was as though the parking lot didn't even exist. Or it was a conspiracy being kept from us.

I could barely concentrate in my classes. I wanted the end of the day to come so badly it hurt. I had doodled most of day away and, embarrassingly, even drew a few hearts over my letter "I"'s.

At lunch, Abby was sitting with her new BFF Sara. It didn't really look welcoming so I carried my tray to an empty nearby table. I was certain I was going to wind up eating lunch alone, which was a far cry from feeling like I was on the road to popularity.

As soon as I plopped my tray down, a sandy-haired girl walked up and sat with a bagel and a knife, butter packets and a napkin.

"I'm Fiona. I'm on the school paper. Can I sit here?"

"Sure," I said.

Fiona looked like a Fiona. Not in the Shrek way but in the other way. My mom had old CDs around the house by an old singer named Fiona. I always thought that was such an amazingly cool name.

I bit into an apple and tried not to look over at Abby and Sara. CRUNCH.

"Why are you sitting alone anyway?" Fiona asked and started spreading butter on her bagel.

"Why not," I said, pretty uninvitingly.

"Aren't you part of MASCARA or something? Don't you sit with older girls?"

I started fussing with my hair a little with my spare hand. CRUNCH.

Fiona just continued to stare at me.

CRUNCH.

"Look, I've been trying to write a story on MASCARA for two years. Would you be open to answering some questions?" she asked.

"No," I said flatly.

"Why not?" she asked. "Do they tell you not to?"

She started to retrieve a notebook from her bag.

CRUNCH.

I was quickly beginning to not like Fiona.

As I looked up, I saw "him" in the way back of the lunchroom. Derek Mackey. Derek "Macs." He didn't have lunch this period. What the Hell was he doing here?

"Um, no, no nothing like that," I said to Fiona, all the while not breaking my gaze.

Geez. There he was. In all his glory. He was standing at a soda machine. Even the way he waited for a soda can was different. I watched as two boys walked up to him and they exchanged hand slaps or pounds or whatever it is boys do. That half hug. What is that anyway?

Fiona turned around to meet my gaze.

"Derek Mackey?" she asked.

"What, no," I said a little too defensively.

"Look, I don't mean to be rude but I'm just not interested in sharing my life in the newspaper. Thanks anyway," I said.

"Suit yourself," Fiona said.

She zipped up her bag and began to leave, bagel in hand.

"So that's it? That's why you sat with me?"

"Why else would I sit with you, you're a freshman eating alone."

I couldn't believe it. What was wrong with this school?

Great. Alone again. CRUNCH.

I propped my head on my hand and tried not to look like I was staring. I also tried not to look like I was eating alone. I should get up and walk away. To the vending machine or even the bathroom. I had at least 15 minutes left to endure this humiliation and I was not going to let Derek Mackey see me eating lunch alone.

I wasn't even hungry anymore.

I underhandly threw my apple core in a nearby garbage can, grabbed my things and started for the door. Just as I was about to empty my tray, out of the corner of my eye I could see Derek leaving. It was as though he had his own private VIP lunch roped off somewhere.

I wasn't the only one watching him leave the lunchroom. A nearby table of girls giggled. Like actually giggled. This day was getting worse by the minute.

Think of the senior parking lot. Think of Asher's car. You are getting a ride home from Asher Sutherland. None of this matters.

I was almost out of the lunchroom when...

"Hey, you're Jorie Carr right?" a very tall and built boy asked.

"Maybe," I said, not really wanting to do this song and dance anymore.

"I'm Liam. Are you going to the game Friday night?"

"Ugh. I don't know. I don't know okay," I snapped.

With that, I walked out of the lunchroom.

My face felt hot.

Finally. Freedom from people.

I went to the girl's bathroom and locked myself into a stall. I didn't want to talk to anyone. For a second, I felt like crying but it passed as quickly as it came. Why was I even upset? I felt around my bag for my phone. No new messages since Asher's text.

I sat in the stall and played a quick game on my phone to distract me from everything that was going on. What I should have been doing was studying for an eighth period quiz but instead I was shooting birds over a wall.

I started thinking about the MASCARA app. What could it do? How did Asher's Dad create an app? I mean, how does anyone create an app?

I was lost in my thoughts (surprise) when I heard two girls walk in the bathroom. I decided to just sit there. I had at least ten minutes to kill before next period and I didn't feel like getting asked any questions.

"Which one do you like?" the one girl said.

There was a pause. Like someone was putting on lipstick or something.

"Mmmm, not really sure yet," the other girl answered.

I could smell smoke. Cigarette smoke definitely. I peered through the small crack between the stall doors.

I could see dangling legs hanging off of the sink and another pair of stocking-ed legs standing. They were definitely smoking a cigarette, right there in the open.

"We need one to drop early on so let me know who you don't like and I'll work on it," the first girl said.

The girl with her back to me cocked her head back and blew a puff of gray air toward the windows. They must have opened them. It felt a little chilly.

I tried hard not to move. Not to make a sound so they didn't know I was in there.

"Jorie is Asher's pet so you know she's untouchable," the other girl replied after an exhalation.

Was I delusional? They were talking about me.

I squinted harder through the crack and made out Mara French's Chanel bag on the sink and the back of Amanda Betancourt's half-up hairdo.

"Oh my God I know. What is it with her and that girl?" Mara said.

Don't move, don't move, don't move.

Amanda passed the cigarette back to Mara.

"I don't know but it's serious and you know how Asher gets," Amanda said.

Mara exhaled. "Asher gets what Asher wants," she said. Mara extended the cigarette.

"I don't want anymore, flush it," Amanda said.

Mara scooted off the sink. "Asher picked you and Carmen though. It's like why do we even have a process in place if it's always her bids that cross over?"

"Well, who would you rather see get in?"

"I don't know. I don't know them well enough yet. You know one of them won't be able to hack it after the first task. And if that doesn't break them then Senior Slave day will."

Amanda laughed. "I remember my Senior Slave day. Worst day ever."

"I'm gonna be late. Let's go," Mara said.

And they were gone. I had to move quickly before I wound up getting blamed for a cigarette I didn't even smoke. But I couldn't go too quickly. What if they were right outside? Three minutes to the bell.

Was I really Asher's pet? Was it good to be someone's pet? It sounded like an insult. I wasn't a pet. And I sure didn't want to be favored. What did I get myself into?

Two minutes.

One minute.

Go.

The rest of the day went by in practically slow motion. I saw Derek Mackey exactly two more times, but both times he didn't say a word to me. It was as though we never even shared that moment this morning. One of the two times he was completely surrounded by girls at his locker. All kinds of girls. Girls with hemp necklaces and girls with bob haircuts, girls in a trio and girls with piercings. They were all just there. Swooning and waiting for him to do something like a monkey in a circus.

I also saw Abby at her locker exactly three times and all three times were awkward. I think the most she said to me was "Hey."

That's all I got. "Hey."

I had only been at Saint Lawrence for like two weeks and already everything I knew had been turned upside down. I wasn't sure if it was a good upside down or a bad upside down, all I knew was that I was tired. Instead of thinking about my classes or finding a favorite teacher, all I could think about was how I was going to be allowed to sleep at Asher's if I had to work at the store and what was Senior Slave Day and somehow I had to remember things like pep rallies and Halloween Dances and tasks and football games. High school was beginning to get complicated and I was never one for complicated.

Right then, I saw Asher. Standing at the edge of the senior hallway in a headband that actually made her hair look more perfect than normal. If I wore a headband I'd look like I was four. Or jogging.

"Marjorie, you got my text!"

Did she really just call me that in public?

There was nothing I could do. If she wanted to call me Phil I probably wouldn't correct her. Damn. I was her pet.

I smiled.

"Yes!"

She didn't look as smiley. In fact, she looked like she was mad.

"Perfect. Let's go," she said.

I followed. I walked through the senior hallway right behind her. I may as well have been on a leash.

A lot of seniors took notice of me for that minute. Either that or they were just staring at her. I didn't care.

We walked out the back door to the parking lot, all of the bare parts of my legs got goosebumps.

I watched as everyone congregated around cars. All the good little boys and girls in their stiff uniforms began peeling their layers off, stepping out of the demerits and rules and throwing on human clothes. No more polos or oxfords, girls were actually changing in their cars. Boys were taking their shirts off and sitting on the backs of trucks and cars. A few people lit cigarettes. No one looked like they were in a rush to go home. It was a beautiful day outside. A perfect September day.

We zig-zagged through the lot and finally stopped at a white Mini Cooper. I wondered all day what kind of car Asher drove. Embarrassingly.

I walked to the passenger side and put my hand on the door.

"Hang out a minute," Asher said.

She opened her back door and fished a blouse out of her back seat. There were more clothes in her backseat than I had in my closet.

"Okay," I obliged.

I felt silly to still be in uniform while it appeared no one was any longer.

Asher expertly maneuvered her school shirt off and her blouse on through one strategic sleeve move that I knew if I tried I would clumsily pull a muscle. She pulled the headband out of her hair and slipped a huge pair of sunglasses on her face. Then we just sort of stood. Out of the corner of my eye I saw Derek Mackey sitting on the back of a Jeep but I refused to look look.

"So this is the senior parking lot," I said. As soon as I said it I kind of regretted how green I sounded.

"Yep, pretty cool huh," Asher answered.

"Beats the bus," I said trying to sound all James Dean.

"Do you smoke?"

"Me, no," I said.

There goes James Dean.

"Good," she said. "Sometimes I'll have one at a party or if I am drinking a beer but I really don't drink. It just seems so juvenile," she said.

Weren't we juveniles?

"I hear ya," I said. "Totally juvenile."

"If you're going to drink, drink wine. Don't drink beer. It's unbecoming."

Check.

"Sometimes I have a glass of my mom's left over wine with my friend Abby but I'm not sure I love red wine," I said honestly.

"Drink white," Asher said. "You'll like it more."

Asher's phone was already ringing. Not even three minutes out of school and people were already calling her. The only person that ever called me was my mom.

She ignored the call. She ignored the call for me.

"I'm going to get a bottle of strawberry wine for when you sleep over this weekend," she said. "Do you like strawberry?"

Her phone began to ring again. I so badly wished my phone would ring.

"Sure," I said. I'd drink asparagus wine with her if she had it.

"Did you ask your mom if you can come?" she asked.

"Asher!" someone yelled.

I saw Mara heading towards us; she looked so different after hours.

"Incoming," Asher warned.

I was grateful I didn't have to answer whether I had asked my mom yet. I had no idea what I was going to do if she said no. I always worked eight hour shifts at the water store on Saturdays and Sundays. Sixteen hours a week, every week. They were very committed to that schedule. It also kept me making about 300 bucks a week, most of which I saved.

Mara reached us. I never really realized how amazing her facial features were. I wasn't even entirely sure I liked her but I had to admit, she was extremely pretty. Maybe puzzle pretty. She had skin like porcelain.

"Hey, we haven't formally met yet. I'm Mara," she said and put out her hand. "I was a little tied up in my Robbie this morning."

I shook it, kind of weakly. She failed to mention she was completely rude this morning.

"Jorie," I said.

"Are you driving her home?" Mara asked Asher.

"Yea," Asher said.

"Oh. Okay. Are we not going to Soul Cycle today?"

"I have to take care of something. Can we reschedule?"

I felt like I was somehow ruining something.

Mara shrugged. "That's fine. I have to catch up on two podcasts anyway. There are so many good bands coming out at the same time. Did you know that The Teachers are already on their sophomore album?"

Asher laughed. "Is The Teachers really the name of a band? Never heard of 'em," Asher said.

"That's why you have me," said Mara.

"True," Asher replied, sweetly.

Mara looked satisfied. "Always," she said.

"Always," Asher said.

I didn't know what they were talking about. Bands I didn't know but wanted to know. Inside jokes I wanted to be inside of.

"Are you ready?" Asher asked me. Her phone was actually ringing again. Was anyone really this popular in real life?

I got inside her car. There were a hundred things I could and should be thinking about but the only thing I really cared about in this moment was that I was sitting shotgun in Asher Sutherland's car. That people were going to see me pulling out of the senior parking lot in not just any senior's car but Asher's Mini Cooper. What a rush.

I watched as the line of dingy busses slowly pulled out of the front of the school in front of us. I thought of Abby sitting on the bus and for a brief second I felt a twinge of guilt.

"What's your address," Asher interrupted my guilt.

"40 Copperfield Place," I said, robotically.

She nodded and with one hand plugged this into a GPS.

"So. Derek Mackey," Asher said.

Right to the chase. No small talk.

I just nodded.

"He's trouble," Asher said flatly.

"Trouble how?" I asked.

"He's a first and last name guy," Asher said.

"A what now?"

Don't we all have first and last names? Was he supposed to go by a single name like Ricardo (roll the "r") or something? He didn't look like a Ricardo.

"A first and last name guy," Asher repeated.

She carefully steered the car and accelerated.

"How many times have you said his name?" she asked. "Honestly."

I didn't know if this was a trick question and I certainly didn't want to sound like a stalker. I had exchanged two words with the boy, both of which were said by him, might I add.

"Once or twice," I said.

"In your head counts too," Asher said.

I froze. In my head? A thousand. Just today.

"Four?" I lied.

"Okay you're totally lying but nevertheless," Asher said. "Have you called him Derek any of those times? Just Derek?"

I thought about this for a second.

"No?"

"Exactly," she said proudly and brought the car to a stop at a light.

She continued. "There are first name guys, there are last name guys and then there are first and last name guys."

"I don't follow," I said.

"I know. That's why I'm driving you home, to explain it. First name guys, like guys you just call Billy or Ben from Science class, are nice guys. They're the guys you want to tell your parents about. Last name guys, a guy you'd call Beckett or McCoy, they're immature. Or jocks. Usually both. They're the guys that crush beer cans on their heads."

I laughed.

"But a guy that you say his first and last name *every* time you talk about him, even in your head, is a heart breaker," Asher finished.

She concentrated on the road.

I let this theory digest for a minute.

"Everyone calls Derek Mackey, Derek Mackey. Funny thing is, they always call Rob Mackey 'Rob' and we just call Adrianna 'Macs.'"

Asher turned when the GPS told her to. We were coming closer to my street.

"Besides, you can't date while you pledge anyway and forget what dating Macs' brother would do to the program right now," Asher said.

"I don't even know if he likes me, he doesn't even know me," I protested.

"Honey, you're rushing MASCARA. Everyone likes you right now. And everyone is going to want to date you," Asher said, pulling onto my block.

"I'm not trying to sound rude but don't people *always* call you Asher Sutherland, like every time they mention you?"

Asher looked at me and parked the car. She smiled.

"I never claimed I wasn't a heartbreaker," she said.

I unclicked my seatbelt. We were in front of my house.

"So, you're gonna ask your mom right? Would it help if she met me?"

I hadn't told my mom anything yet.

"If it comes to that I'll let you know," I said. "Thanks for the ride. And the advice."

I grabbed my bag and started to get out of her car.

"Anytime sweetie. You should come to the football game Friday. Cheer Sue on," Asher said. She didn't wait for an answer. She just took off.

Despite how much I liked being called sweetie, I didn't like that Derek Mackey was off limits. I absolutely hated when people told me something was off limits. Cake, cookies, ice cream, boys, didn't matter – it only made you want them more.

I trudged inside where I knew my mom and Matt would be waiting to dissect me. Like a frog lying on my back. I mean, I got dropped off in someone's car, what did I expect?

I fished for my keys and opened the front door. I could have gone through the garage but I thought I'd have an easier time avoiding them if I went through the front. I was wrong.

"Who was that girl honey?"

Really?

I was in no mood for the Spanish Inquisition.

"A friend. Asher is her name. She is helping me with one of my classes," I lied.

I really was becoming quite the liar.

"How old is she?" my mom asked, while she continued to read whatever it was she was reading.

"I don't know, she's a senior," I offered.

"Why didn't you just take the bus?"

"I told you, she's helping with one of my classes."

"Which one?" my mom asked.

"Biology," I said quickly. Almost too quickly. Like I'd been storing it in my head for such an occasion. Truthfully, it was the upside down dissected frog that made me think of it.

"Ooh, Jorie is riding in cars!" my brother Matt chimed from in front of the television. Like two inches in front of the television, how he always sat.

"So?" I quipped, not at all nicely.

"Why is she helping you?" my mom continued.

"Because she's a nice person," I said and started for the staircase. I needed my room. And a very shut door.

"Speaking of Asher, she is going to help me out this weekend too. I have a football game to go to and then I may spend the night. I'll still work at the store on Saturday don't worry," I called while halfway up the stairs.

"We're not done talking about this Marjorie," my mom called back.

She only called me Marjorie when it was necessary.

I threw my things down and grabbed a handful of those make-up wipe things from my vanity counter. I had to rub the blue off my eyes before dinner. I was lucky my mom didn't look up and see them yet. Just another conversation I didn't feel like having.

It took like four wipes to get all the cobalt off my eyes. I looked like the Cookie Monster. I sighed and flopped on my bed. All I wanted was to stare at my ceiling for the next two hours. I don't know why I felt so overdramatic nor did I know why I thought staring at my ceiling helped but somehow, it did.

I grabbed a set of earphones and plugged into my phone. I should know bands like The Teachers If I was really going to follow through with this.

I found a few songs of theirs and clicked play on one at random. I had every intention of drifting off when Derek Mackey ran himself right back into my head.

Damn it.

He was just so incredibly intriguing.

Why did Asher have such an issue with me having a crush on him? I can have a crush on whomever I choose. Couldn't I?

Stop thinking about Derek Mackey. Stop calling him Derek Mackey. Even in your head.

CHAPTER 7

"Peps and Pets"

I had the weirdest dream last night and by morning I still couldn't shake it. My dream was that Asher was famous and I was her Chihuahua. You know the kind, with the rhinestone collar tucked into an oversized bag and toted around Hollywood. I couldn't talk (because I was a dog) but I had human thoughts and I wanted to tell her to let me out of that damn bag. Then all the other girls in MASCARA walked around her like an entourage and one by one they "oohed" and "awed" at me and even pet me.

I woke up in a sweaty panic. I also woke up to a monster size pimple right smack in the middle of my forehead. Perfect. What was it I was supposed to do? Not pop it but put toothpaste on it? That seemed like the single most ridiculous thing I had ever heard. Well, second only to being someone's pet Chihuahua in their oversized pocketbook.

This morning was turning out to be a disaster.

And today was the pep rally. So I got to be the freshman who stood out as the bright eyelash-ed puppy with a pimple. To make matters worse, I was getting my first pledge task tonight and I didn't really feel up to the challenge. I smeared a small dab of minty fresh toothpaste over the crater on my face and tried to make the most of my uniform. I couldn't wear out the accessories I had bought the other day, otherwise I would just look desperate.

My dad flew in last night and forged some meaningless conversation while drinking his coffee this morning like we always did. I was tired and grouchy, he was pensive and serious.

"Your mom tells me that a senior is helping you with your Science class. I didn't know you had a problem with Science."

Well Dad, I don't except I've morphed into a pet Chihuahua overnight and I cannot seem to figure out the sheer science of toothpaste on a pimple.

Instead I said, "Yea."

I ate my cereal in silence other than my "yea."

He read the newspaper. Then sipped. My mom got Matt ready for school. Rinse and repeat.

I walked to the bus stop afraid of what the rest of the day held. It was starting to get a little chilly out.

Abby was at the bus stop talking to a boy. What universe was this?

He looked like he was super into whatever she was saying. I somehow became the third wheel waiting in an awkward group for the big yellow hunk of crap to pull up.

Then I overheard the thing that really propelled my morning over the line.

"Did you hear that Joe Devaney was expelled?"

This phrase did a somersault in my head. Joe Devaney was the very reason I signed up for the insanity that was Saint Lawrence.

I couldn't help myself.

"What? He did?" I asked.

Abby looked coldly at me.

"I heard yesterday," she said to both me and Bus Stop Boy.

"And you didn't tell me?" I exclaimed.

Bus Stop Boy looked taken aback.

"You know Joe Devaney?" he asked, a little too perplexed.

I didn't know how to answer that. I did, well sort of, know Joe. In the I-signed-up-for-Catholic-school-without-really-knowing-you-but-because-of-you kind of way.

Abby answered for me.

"Know him? Jorie is positively in love with Joe! She made us come to this wonderful school because of him!"

Did that just happen?

Bus Stop Boy looked embarrassed for me.

As luck would have it, the bus pulled to a screechy stop in front of our really Reality TV moment.

I looked at Bus Stop Boy but it was too late. He would believe anything Abby said at this point. They sat together in an uncomfortable two seater even though there were plenty of empty seats. And Joe Devaney was apparently expelled. Amazing.

The worst part was that even though I was sad to hear the news about Joe, I was partly so immersed in this whole Derek Mackey first name last name heartbreaker that I didn't even know if I cared anymore.

I rode the bus in complete silence. In fact, I, embarrassingly, looked up how many followers Asher Sutherland had on social media. Yes, I was a Chihuahua I know. But I had to cyberstalk. I just had to. And do you know how many followers she had?

4,057. Four *thousand* and fifty-seven. Do you know how many I had? Like 200. I know this was of course the most irrelevant fact of all irrelevant facts in the grand scheme of life but I'd be lying if I said I wasn't jealous. Jealous in the I" wanted four thousand followers" kind of way.

As soon as I got to homeroom I noticed something was off. At first I couldn't figure out what it was. It couldn't have anything to do with Joe

Devaney since I hadn't known he was gone for the last two weeks so really what difference did it make now?

I turned around in my desk to lock eyes with Anders Cavelli. She looked different. I surveyed her uniform but it looked perfectly normal. Then it hit me.

She wasn't wearing the blue mascara.

I didn't have her number and still to this day hadn't exchanged more than three words with her so I wasn't sure how to ask her why. But I had to know.

I waited for the bell to ring but fidgeted at my desk the entire time. I fidgeted with my hair, with a compact mirror, with a notebook, with a pen cap, whatever I could find.

Then, as soon as the class let out, I nearly tackled the kid in front of me to race for the door.

"Anders," I said breathy.

She looked at me in a "what" kind of way.

"You forgot to wear the mascara," I said, even though I had a gut feeling it was no accident. "You can borrow mine if you need to."

"That won't be necessary. I've decided to drop."

Drop? What? Why?

"You what?" I blurted out.

"It's not the end of the world," she said plainly.

"I, I know," I said.

But it was the end of the world. Why would she elect to do something like that?

The worst part was, that somewhere in me I was secretly kind of glad. It meant that now I was only competing against four girls for two open slots. And let's face it, Anders wasn't exactly being the friendliest person on Earth right now.

"I'm sorry to hear that," I lied.

"I'm sure you are," she retorted.

I didn't know what to say. I decided to walk off before I was late to class.

I wanted to grab a book out of my locker beforehand and noticed another blue card had been slipped inside.

Jorie—

As you may have heard, one pledge has decided to drop. Her loss. Tonight will be your first task. Meet us after the pep rally for a quick "pep talk" if you will. We can give you more direction then.

Always,
Mara

I folded it up back into the envelope and tucked it into my bag. Abby, Sara, and Bus Stop Boy surrounded Abby's locker. I didn't even care anymore if they were looking at me. Let them look.

I wondered why Mara wrote this card and not Asher but I couldn't pay it that much attention. I wanted to keep focused on my classes today and distract myself from whatever this "task" was tonight at the game.

Just when I thought I was safe, I spotted Derek Mackey. Damn it, Derek. Just Derek.

He was walking toward me. So much for focus.

This couldn't be happening. This most certainly was happening. Not far from Abby's locker either. Great.

"Jorie right?" he said. He smelled like a department store counter. I couldn't help but know that whatever that cologne was, it would bring me to him in my mind forever after this moment.

Keep cool Jorie.

"Yes," was all I said.

Did I pretend I didn't know who he was? Was that the cool way to play this?

"Derek Mackey, nice to finally meet you," he said.

"Oh right, Adrianna's brother. Nice to meet you too," I said.

His eyes were amazing. His everything was amazing. *Stop it.*

"You going to the football game tonight?" he asked.

If he asked me to the moon I would go.

"I think so," I lied. Of course I was.

"Cool, maybe I'll see you tonight then," he said.

I'm having a conversation with Derek Mackey. I'm having a conversation with Derek Mackey. I'm having a conversation with Derek Mackey.

I really hoped this would get easier as time went on.

"Sounds good," I said.

I mentally patted myself on the back for a conversation well played. I think.

But I still hadn't left. I was still standing there. He just had to be the one who walked away first. I knew he would be.

"Later Jorie," Derek said.

I noticed Abby out of the very corner of my eye.

She thought I didn't see her pretending not to see me but I was pretending not to see her, pretending not to see me.

I had to get to class.

I'm pretty sure I had only one minute to the bell when I brushed past Rachel Whitley, in her pedigreed perfectness.

She smiled. A genuine smile. Then she leaned in to whisper.

"The toothpaste goes on the pimple overnight. I think you left some on and I can still see the green."

No no no no no.

"Thanks," I whispered back.

I blushed. Definitely. Then licked my thumb and ran it over the life-form on my forehead. I licked my thumb again and could taste my minty fresh mistake.

That's when it really hit me. I just had my first conversation with Derek Mackey and I had toothpaste on my head. This so could not be happening.

I hoped that I was still dreaming. Maybe I was first a Chihuahua but then I was at school dreaming of pimples and toothpaste and talks with Derek Mackey. Damn it, Derek. Just Derek.

I'm not dreaming. At least I don't think I am.

Time for class.

I was pretty sure my History teacher hated me by now. I was in dangerous territory for getting a detention and it was only the first month. It was really hard not to be late to the first class of the day, so much hustle and bustle after homeroom. I fell prey to it everyday.

I was still buzzing from the Derek conversation, even if I had tooth-paste on my head. Maybe he didn't see it. Maybe the lighting was in my favor?

"Pop quiz everyone, I hope you've been paying attention," said Mr. Walsh.

And the day from Hell continues.

I wondered if I brought up a day from Hell in next period's Religion class if my teacher would be upset or embrace it as a yearning for knowledge.

Hell hath bestowed upon Marjorie Carr a day of its very own kind filled with fire and sin.

Nah, she'd probably be upset.

I started to wonder what Joe Devaney did to get expelled. But my thoughts were soon interrupted by a ten question quiz of which I knew one answer.

Why couldn't I have paid attention to the Battle of Bunker Hill? I knew that was a terrible decision.

I clicked and unclicked my pen to the point where I knew it was distracting people and quickly stopped.

"Twenty minutes left," Mr. Walsh warned. I swear he looked right at me.

I felt like a flopping dying fish.

I was really good at school in middle school. I got exceptionally good grades and rarely ever got in trouble. I'm sure it was all the recent drama that had me flopping.

I tried to put down answers that sounded like they could be right but let's face it, there was no way to fudge history, it either happened that way or it didn't. It was pretty set in stone.

I was sure my made-up answers were making historical figures everywhere turn over in their graves. I was botching heroic feats and infamous wars.

I started to picture a soldier about to load gunpowder into a cannon and stopping. "What is Marjorie Carr *doing* to this battle?" My black and white vision of World War I veterans making fun of me took over my remaining 19 minutes and—

"That's it class, please put your pens down and pass your papers up," said Mr. Walsh.

Daydreamed the class away. As usual.

I half-groaned and handed my paper to the girl in front of me face down so she couldn't see my ridiculously dumb answers.

It was time for Religion class where I could get a better grip on Hell. Less than six hours until the pep rally.

I was almost out the door when I heard, "Ms. Carr, may I suggest that whatever is distracting you in my class become a part of your own history? I haven't failed anyone in a long time and I don't intend to start this year."

"Yes, thank you," was all I could muster up. If he only knew.

CHAPTER 8

"Go Knights"

The pep rally was the most surreal thing I had ever seen. You don't realize how big your school is until everyone is stuffed into the same place. It looked like tens of thousands of people even though I knew it was likely only two thousand. We went after seventh period and I hadn't made any plans on where I was going to sit. I wasn't even sure what it would all look like until I got inside and saw the overstuffed risers.

As luck would have it, I was walking in right around the same time as Carmen Banks and who I could only guess was her sister. They looked a lot alike. Dark skin with such contrasting blue-green eyes that looked like contacts. I knew they weren't but it was hard to believe anyone was honestly blessed with that coloring. Mercedes didn't dress nearly as good as Carmen did.

"Oh hey Jorie. This is Mercedes," she said as we filed into the rows.

I smiled at the girl. "Hey, I'm Jorie," I said.

The girl looked at my eyelashes instead of my smile.

"Oh hi. Are you pledging MASCARA?"

I didn't say anything.

Carmen took over for me. "She is. Her real name is Marjorie."

Zing. I may as well wear a nametag by now. Hi, my name is Marjorie. I wear toothpaste on my forehead and yes that is a zit.

Mercedes didn't say anything. Neither did I.

We walked over to two empty spots on the bleachers and sat.

Not even thirty seconds later, Carmen got up to run over to Amanda and Rachel. I hung my head in shame when I saw Rachel, beyond embarrassed over our earlier encounter.

Mercedes must have noticed my ducking.

"Not fan of which, Amanda or Adrianna?" she asked.

"Oh, no it's not that. I honestly don't know them well enough to be a, fan or not a fan or whatever," I said.

"Well let me give you the basic run down; MASCARA cliff notes. Adrianna is the partying one, blessed with two good looking siblings and once a month there's like sixty people over their house. I'm sure you've heard of a Macs party," she started.

I hoped to God my face didn't give anything away. "Yea," I said.

"Amanda is the bitchy one. Although, when you get to know her, she's not that bad. Tough one might be a better way to describe her."

Good to know.

"My sister as you know is the eccentric one. Queen of all things fashion. She gets that from our mother. And aunt."

She said aunt like "ont" which I always loved. I said it like "ant." Like the bug. Bleagh.

"Rachel comes from old money and it's pretty obvious. They still do the Roman numeral thing in her family if you know what I mean."

I nodded. I think I knew what she meant.

"Sue is exactly what you picture when you think of the ditzy 'that girl' in high school. But she knows, like, every parent and every coach and everyone in the community so she gets MASCARA involved in tons of philanthropies and raises good money."

Mercedes pointed to the girl I assumed was Sue now standing on the sidelines of the gym floor. She did look like the 'that girl' you think of when you think of high school cheerleaders.

"Mara is the sensitive one. Knows her music but between you and I, I think she's always been a tad jealous of Asher. And well, you know Asher. Queen Bee. Sometimes, the manipulative one. That girl is just so damn used to getting what she wants."

I had this hard bubble in the back of my throat when she said that. Manipulative was never a very good personality trait. Then again, what Asher wanted, was for me to get in to MASCARA. I half-smiled.

"Did you want to join?" I asked blatantly.

Mercedes paused for a second. "At first, yea. Who doesn't? But after seeing it through Carmen for a while, I realized it wasn't a fit for me. Don't tell her I told you that. She would have cut off her right arm to have gotten me in. And I honestly appreciate that."

"Hmm," was all I said.

Carmen and Rachel were looking our way so I decided to look off into the distance. Somehow, amid thousands of blurred bodies and smooshed students, I could actually spot Derek Mackey all the way across the entire gymnasium. He had a white fleece sweatshirt pulled over his uniform shirt. He was laughing and basically glowing. He might as well have been glowing anyway.

All this blah maroon and there he was popping out of the crowd in bright white and smiles. Why was he so happy? No one was that damn happy.

Carmen scooted back into her seat just as the pep rally was getting underway.

There were all sorts of banging noises on the bleachers and commotion once it started. Since this was my first, I just sort of kept quiet and tried my hardest not to look over at Derek. Our mascot was a knight, how very fairy tale. The cheerleaders chanted their praise to the Saint

Lawrence Knights and I watched Sue be bubbly like a good little subject in the MASCARA court. Then my A.D.D got the better of me…

I started to envision Asher in a queen's robe sitting high on a throne and annunciating her words, like she does, to her jester— which was of course me. There I was in purple and red striped jester garb trying to juggle, which I am not good at at all, and trying to please her. She turns to the King, which is obviously Derek Mackey, and tells him she is displeased but all he can do is smile.

"This jester isn't amusing me my Lord, I want a new one," she'd say.

He ignores the fact that I am dropping all of the balls that I am trying so hard to keep in this cyclical motion around my head but the monkey with cymbals is doing a much better job than I am.

"My Lord, let's keep the monkey and behead the jester," she'd conclude.

"Very well my Queen," he'd respond.

Then I am hauled off to my imminent death but first they'll starve me in some dungeon downstairs.

My imagination kept me in the royal nightmare for at least twenty minutes. I was missing so much of the pep in everyone's step.

"Jorie. Jorie," Carmen said.

I had a sinking feeling she was saying my name for awhile.

"Huh? What?" I said.

"Let's start making our way down before everyone else and find your fellow pledges," Carmen answered.

Fellow pledges? Was I still hallucinating?

Nope.

"Okay," I answered.

I grabbed my things and followed Carmen as she maneuvered her way below right through the hoopla and "Go Knights."

"Have you met Sue yet?" she asked me as we shimmied our way south.

"No, I haven't," I said.

"Okay, let me try to find her," Carmen said.

I watched as her accessories jingled and jangled and studied the many pieces of, just things, that she put on every morning. Did she take all of this stuff off at night? How very exhausting.

"Sue!" she called to the front and center cheerleader while her jangly skinny arm shook.

Sue looked up and started walking over.

They were announcing all of the football players so maybe her part was done.

"This is Jorie Carr," Carmen said to Sue when she reached us.

I was really thankful she called me Jorie.

"It's nice to meet you," I said to her.

"Hey Jorie! It's so nice to meet you! Did you enjoy the rally?"

Oh my God she was so friendly.

"Yes, it was so cool," I said enthusiastically, knowing that 'No, I ignored most of it and pictured a kingdom of nonsense' was not going to work here.

I smiled. She smiled. Everyone was very smiley today. Pep.

Except for the looming feeling that I had a task to do tonight and was dreading what it was.

Right then, Andy Flynn walked up and joined our half circle. It was so awful to think this but I was relieved that she didn't pose a threat to me since she was an "A" and I was going for the "M" spot. Then again, since Anders dropped today, Andy was a shoe-in for the "A" spot and that made me very, irrationally jealous.

"Have you girls met?" Sue asked Andy and I.

"Not really," I said honestly. "Kind of."

"No," said Andy.

"This is Marjorie, Marjorie this is Andy," Carmen offered.

"Hey," she said.

"Hey," I responded.

There was an awkward pause.

"Why did Anders Cavelli drop?" Andy asked, pretty unapologetically.

Thank God she asked because I certainly didn't want to.

Carmen looked at Sue, Sue looked at Carmen. No one wanted to answer and that was beyond obvious. I shot a look at Andy that basically said, "whatever they tell us is going to be a lie anyway."

"She was scared. Plain and simple," Carmen finally decided on.

"We always get drops before the first task. They chicken out," Sue added.

"Obviously she wasn't MASCARA material," Carmen said.

Andy looked proud that she was still here. I on the other hand was starting to sweat. Was I MASCARA material?

"Cameron!" a boy's voice called out to Sue. We all looked.

It was Derek and another boy I hadn't yet seen.

Sue smiled a big cheerleader smile.

"Hey Stern," she called back to them.

"See ya at the game tonight gorgeous," the boy called Stern said.

"Yup. Go Knights," she replied.

Derek looked right at me. Of this, I was 100 percent certain. Not at Andy, not at Carmen, not at Sue. He looked dead at me. I froze.

It was like staring at a Medusa head. Completely powerless. Ugh, what was it about this boy?

I was sure I was going to get snagged by one of the girls but none of them caught this delicious exchange. It was as though I paused time, had a moment with Derek, and then unpaused time and everything went back to normal. Whatever normal was anymore.

He even glanced one last time over his shoulder. I may imagine a lot of things but I was not imagining this.

I would never admit it to anyone, but I felt a high after that like I had never before known was even possible. Like all the other drama just melted away and I could breathe on that moment like oxygen for the next 12 hours. It was mortifying, but it was true. He had changed my entire mood with one look. Because I knew it was for me and I knew it was unspoken and it didn't have to be a single thing more than that. Not yet.

"Well, I'm up for the challenge," I said, suddenly changing my entire tune.

"That's the spirit Jorie. That's what MASCARA's are made of," Sue said.

She didn't know where I got my wings from but as far as I was concerned, she didn't need to know.

Missy Warwick, bragger extraordinaire, joined us. So did Mara and Amanda.

"What are you ladies chattin' about?" asked Mara.

Wow, she certainly *was* the sensitive one! I hadn't seen it before but now I did.

"How are these bitches getting home?" Carmen joked to Mara and Amanda as they approached.

"I'm not takin' 'em. Let Mara and Asher figure that out. That's their responsibility," Amanda said. I couldn't tell if she was serious or kidding. My guess was serious.

"Shush. I'll take three of them and Asher can take the other two," Mara said.

"Where are the rest of you?' Mara asked to, I assume, me.

"Oh, I'm not sure," I answered.

I really hoped no one was looking at the giant pimple on my head.

"Megan is on her way," Andy said.

"It's fine now, but soon you guys will have to know where all of you are at all times. And I mean *all*," Amanda said.

She was slightly scaring me.

"We should exchange numbers," I said, hoping to score points.

"You guys haven't even done that yet?" Amanda asked.

So much for points. She was Contact Chair. She probably thought we were socially inept to have not done this already.

"We were planning on doing it here," I quickly lied.

Andy shot me a look that may or may not have said 'thank you' and Missy pulled out her phone.

Asher and Megan Welsh walked up behind all of us. I felt strangely bothered that Asher was with Megan. Damn it, I was the pet. I was the cat jealous of the dog.

"Whatcha girls doin'?" Asher asked.

"Exchanging numbers," Missy and I said in unison.

Andy grabbed her phone.

Megan, quick to act, started to get her phone too.

We were all a little pathetic but I was too far gone to care.

Rachel and Adrianna finally appeared with Ashley Walker. We were all here...

"Girls, we'll see you tonight at 7:30. Don't worry yourself with why Anders dropped. It's a waste of time. Finish getting each other's numbers. Jorie and Ashley you're with me, the rest of you go with Mara," Queen Asher beckoned.

Mara wrinkled her face.

"Megan, Missy and Andy, come with me when you're done," she obliged.

All Hail the Queen.

CHAPTER 9

"It's Biology"

We dropped Ashley off first but I got shotgun. It's the little things I guess. We pulled up to my house and Asher shut the car off.

"Should I meet your mom? Did she give you an answer on tonight?"

I wasn't sure how to play this. My mom never did give me a straight answer but I knew for sure she was going to ask Asher about the Science "help" she was giving me. I thought about briefing her on it and then figured if I could rush her in and out of my house fast enough, my mom wouldn't have time to pry.

"Sure, couldn't hurt," I decided out loud.

Asher fixed her hair in the mirror. Why? I don't know. She clicked off her seatbelt.

"Great let's go," she said.

I went in through the garage this time so I could give my mom and Matt thirty seconds to prep before meeting Asher.

"I'm home! Asher's with me," I called out.

Matt popped his head in. He immediately started blushing. My God she even had an effect on nine year olds.

"It's nice to finally meet you," my mom said as she walked in, covered in cake batter. She still had the spoon in one hand and shook Asher's with her spare.

"Mom!" Asher said to my surprise.

She continued. "Well, I feel like you are anyway! Jorie and I have grown so close and she speaks so highly of you. Plus, any mom that bakes is a mom of mine!" Asher said laughing.

My mom was taken with her immediately.

"Really? Jorie just hates baking! Do you want a cupcake?"

"Do I want a cupcake? Is that even a question?"

Asher was good. *Really* good.

Matt pretended he wasn't looking but kept glancing away from the TV and back at us.

"Come in the kitchen, they're fresh," my mom said. She hadn't even spoken to me.

She peeled an icing-heavy cupcake from a tray.

"Here you are," she said and extended the 900 calories to Asher.

"Thanks mom," Asher joked. So corny but it was working.

"You girls have blue on your eyelashes, is that the new trend?"

Uh oh. Cover blown.

I looked down and then decided reaching for a cupcake myself might help deter the questioning.

"Something like that," Asher said and looked at me with a "you haven't told her yet" look on her face.

"For some," I said, which was a half-truth at best.

"I love it, you should put it on me one day Jor," my mom said.

I needed to get Asher out of here and fast.

"Well Asher has a super busy schedule so we don't want to keep her. You're okay with me sleeping over her house tonight right, after the football game?"

"I suppose. What kind of science are you learning?" my mom asked.

"Biology," Asher spit out without even knowing the reason.

Man, this girl was good.

She winked at me when my mom wasn't looking.

"Okay, but be at the store on time tomorrow or your father will be P-I-S-S-E-D," my mom said.

I could not believe she just spelled out "pissed." Embarrassment, I'm Jorie, nice to meet you.

Asher laughed. "What store?"

"Oh Jorie didn't tell you? We own Carr Water Shop over on 63. Jorie works weekends."

"Got it. No problem," I said trying to usher Asher out.

"Oh no kidding! We get our filters there!"

My mom was about to be sold on Asher for life.

Asher finished her cupcake and handed me the paper holder. "See you around seven?"

"Okey doke," I said. I couldn't get her out of there quick enough. It was only a matter of time before my mom broke out baby pictures or fifth grade trophies.

"It was so nice meeting you Mrs. Carr and thank you for the cupcake. It was delicious."

"Anytime," my mom said.

If my mom fell any harder for Asher *she* would be pledging MASCARA soon.

I walked Asher out.

As soon as she was out of earshot she said, "You're welcome."

I laughed. "Biology?"

"I'm quick," she said. "I have to go work off that cupcake now. I would never eat one of those things if it wasn't for you pledging."

She flipped her perfect hair over her shoulder and took off.

I had only four hours to look amazing for the football game. I chucked the other half of my cupcake in the garbage when my mom wasn't looking and ran upstairs to pack.

What does one bring to Asher Sutherland's house? I actually had butterflies in my stomach.

Just as I was surveying my closet and looking for clothes that I could actually wear, my phone rang. It was Abby.

For a split second, I debated whether I should answer it or not. That sounds horrible but I was just so confused by her lately.

I slid the button to pick it up anyway.

"Hello?"

"Jor," she said, she sounded kind of muffled.

"Hey," I said.

I heard a sniffle.

"Did you tell the MASCARA girls to be mean to me?" She sniffled again.

"Did I what? Of course not. Why?"

"Oh. It's just that— nevermind, nothing," she said.

"What do you mean nothing? What happened?" I asked.

I felt my heart starting to beat a little faster. For an instant I had to remind myself that I did nothing of the sort.

"I don't want to cause any trouble. Just forget I mentioned it," she said.

"Abby, tell me what you're talking about," I demanded.

"It's not that big a deal, I just heard some of them picking on me at the pep rally and I thought maybe you were mad at me and told them to," Abby said.

"Who?"

"I'm not sure which. Amanda and Rachel maybe," Abby said.

Not sure which? Abby studied these girls like they were the Bible.

"You don't have to protect them, I know you know who. Was it Amanda and Rachel or not?"

"Yes," she said.

"What were they saying?" I asked.

"Ya know, just making fun of me. The way I walked. The way I wore my hair. Whatever, I'm over it. I just wanted to make sure you didn't have anything to do with it," Abby said.

"Of course I didn't Ab."

"They can be pretty awful," she said. I heard another sniffle.

"I'm sorry that happened to you," I finally said.

"Are you going to the football game with them? She asked.

"Yes, well, with Asher," I said.

"Oh. Well, I'll just stay home then."

"That's silly. You should go."

"Nah. I'm not really feeling up to it. Have fun," Abby said. "I'll see you next week."

She hung up.

This wasn't good.

As mad as I was at Abby, I knew it'd pass. And I had known her for basically my entire life. You take your friend's side when they got picked on. That's just how it goes. But what was I supposed to do here? Say something to Amanda and Rachel?

I was buried on my floor in like fifty pieces of clothing and half-heartedly stuffing overnight things in a duffel bag. Toothbrush, toothpaste (not for my head), pajama pants, t-shirt, magazine (so I kind of looked like I read up on things), face wash. What else did I need? Could I even wear pajama pants at Asher's? She probably slept in like ten thousand count sheets and silk robes.

Should I ask Asher about what happened with Abby? I suddenly felt like there was no one in the world I could talk to. I couldn't talk to Abby about them and I couldn't talk to them about Abby and I couldn't talk to anyone about Derek Mackey and my mom thought I was studying Biology. Mess.

Well, I certainly couldn't have a birthday party next week, since no one seemed to get along.

I felt a little guilty. That's why my mom was making cupcakes. For my birthday. I felt like the worst person in the world. Two days away from fourteen and already the worst person in the world. Like Stalin. Was that his name? I definitely failed my History quiz. Come to think of it, Mr. Walsh hated me too.

My head was hurting. In a matter of hours I had to do my first initiation task for MASACARA and I felt like I just boarded the train to Crazyville.

"Jorie, come eat something before you go!" my mom called up the stairs.

"Coming!'

Didn't my mom understand that I didn't have time to eat? I stood up and let the dozen or so pieces of clothes fall off of my lap. I wanted to wear something bold since we were always stuck in uniforms but my closet was beyond boring. There was nothing here I could even work with. I grabbed an old plaid vest and decided I could possibly make it work with a little help.

I glanced in my mirror covered in pictures of Abby and me. Tons of movie theater strips of us making goofy faces and dumb hand signals.

I felt a pang of bad friendedness.

I had to do something. Somehow stick up for her. I finessed my arms into the sleeve holes of the vest and ran downstairs. My mom and Matt were already eating. My mom was also prepping for wine night.

"Mom *loves* your new friend," my brother said.

"Yep," I said and sat.

We were eating chicken for the four hundred and eighth night in a row. We always ate chicken. Matt scraped his fork across his plate and then shoved a pea in his mouth with his free hand.

"Matt, you liked her too," I said, deciding to toy with him.

"Did not," he said with a beet red face.

My mom laughed.

"Make sure you're on time tomorrow Jor," she said.

"I know," I said.

"So what's with the blue makeup?" my mom asked.

"What do you mean? We told you, it's trendy."

"Really? Because Abby's mom called here an hour ago and said you're joining some kind of sorority?"

The jig was up.

CHAPTER 10

An hour and a half and counting. I decided this wasn't the time or place to come clean about MASCARA. I gave her the old, "I don't know what Abby's talking about. She just doesn't like Asher and her friends."

"What's not to like about Asher?" my mom said.

Exactly.

I put my plate in the sink and ran back upstairs knowing something had to be done about my hair to make up for the enormously erupting volcano on my forehead. I wished I knew what kind of hair products Asher used to get hair to look the way it did. My luck it would wind up being organic berries and waterfall droplets or something. It occurred to me I could peek in her shower tonight or tomorrow and find out.

For now, I had to figure out something and fast. I remembered reading somewhere that you can dye your hair with Kool Aid. I knew we had some because Matt drank Kool Aid from time to time.

A couple pieces couldn't hurt. I ran downstairs and pulled a purple packet from the pantry and ran right back up again so no one would notice what I was doing.

I slowly filled the bathtub with a few inches of lukewarm water and dumped the packet in whole. Careful not to get my vest dirty, I took it off and hung it on the back of the door. I pulled a few select pieces of my mousy hair out and dipped them into the purple water. On the way back up from dunking my hair, I conked the back of my head on the faucet.

Really?

I was dripping purple everywhere and my hair was sticky and all I could taste was sugar. This wasn't going according to plan.

The porcelain of the tub was quickly turning grape. I couldn't keep the pieces of hair I wanted separate from the rest of my head. There was sugar in my scalp and it was close to dripping into my big fat zit. I bet Kool Aid wasn't nearly as good for pimples as toothpaste. This was a disaster. I tried rinsing the pieces in the sink but decided I should just take a full shower at this point. I turned the water on up top and took the rest of my outfit off as fast as I could. The tub was draining but the purple was sticking. I rubbed my feet along the bottom trying to get it to wash away.

A few minutes later I came out of the shower with blue cheeks from my mascara and a few purple hues (if you could call it that) messily mixed into the rest of my head. My pimple basically had it's own talk show by now. And to boot, the bathroom was a mess.

I looked like I got punched in the face by a pack of crayons. Wonderful.

No vest was going to fix this.

Asher pulled up exactly at 7:05. Somehow, I managed to pull myself together by then but it wasn't easy. The bathroom however? Not so successful. I ran out of the house before my mom could notice the damage.

"See you tomorrow!" I yelled.

"Be careful Jorie!" my mom yelled back.

I ran up to the car carrying two bags of crap.

"Cute vest," Asher said when I got in. This somehow made the last two hours of my life worth it.

"Oh thanks, it's old," I said.

"Did you do something different to your hair?"

"No," I answered mortified.

"Oh," Asher said and smiled. "You ready for tonight?"

"Absolutely," I said.

"Good," Asher said.

The car stopped only three blocks from my house. Did we stall?

"Drive," Asher said.

"Wait what?"

"Drive to Saint Lawrence. You can stop a block or two from the school so no one sees you pull in."

"I can't drive, I'm thirteen. I don't even so much as have a permit," I reasoned.

"Neither did I when I did this task. Neither did Mara, or Carmen or—"

"I get it but I literally have no idea how to drive. None."

"Do you want this or not Jorie? C'mon, it's not that hard, and I will guide you through the whole thing. Think of it as a free driving lesson."

"Free driving lesson that's totally and completely illegal."

"Oh lighten up. You're not gonna get pulled over."

"But what if I do? Or worse, what if I crash?"

"You're not gonna crash. Just go slow. And there's a reason we have a Contact Chair. We have every police officer in the county in our contact list. You won't get in trouble for anything ever if you're a MASCARA."

I started to panic. There was no turning back. Or was there? If they made fun of Abby today, did I even want this that bad? It pained me to realize that I did. I wanted this that bad. I unbuckled my seatbelt and opened the passenger door.

"I knew you had it in you!" Asher exclaimed.

I walked slowly around the back of the Mini Cooper. If I am the girl that crashes Asher Sutherland's perfect white car I will never live it down.

Asher ran over to the passenger side.

"Okay, your right foot is on the gas and your left pedal is the brake. You don't need to push down hard. Just slowly lower your foot to go and when you need to brake, you're going to slowly move your right foot to the left pedal and apply pressure to the brake. When you need to make a turn, which there are only two from here to Saint Lawrence, I will help you. You'll just slowly turn the wheel in the direction you're going and then step on the gas. Got it?"

My immediate reaction was no. I didn't know anything she just said. I couldn't even believe I was sitting in the driver's seat of a car. I pushed the thoughts of jail uniforms and prison meals out of my head.

"First, we need to switch the drive out of park to drive, which is the "D."

I could handle that. I took a deep breath and placed my hand on the knob.

"Put your foot on the brake pedal and when you switch to "D," switch your foot to the gas. Slow."

I did what Asher said and the car started moving. Like my grandma was driving, but moving nonetheless. I could not believe I was driving. I swore I felt like the drivers in the other cars on the street could tell that I didn't know what I was doing. Like the oncoming traffic could see all the way into the car, see my face even, and were speed dialing the police to report the license plate of the 13-year old grandmother driver.

"That's good!"

"It is?" I turned toward Asher.

"Keep your eyes on the road!" she yelled.

Oh yeah.

"Sorry," I muttered.

"Okay you have a stop sign coming up. You're going to sloooowly start braking."

I felt like I was learning how to dance and had two left feet. Well, two right feet and no left feet. My left foot wasn't doing anything. Why wasn't my left foot doing anything?!

I took another deep breath. I slowed the car to a stop.

"Perfect. Now press this lever to signal that you're turning. We're gonna make a left."

I clicked the bar down and heard a click-click, click-click, click-click sound.

"Exactly."

I sat there, dumbfounded that this was actually happening.

"Okay, now you need to pull out just a little and make sure there are no cars coming, which it doesn't look there are."

I did what she said. There were no cars anywhere, which was odd for a Friday night on Middle Road.

"Good. Now start turning the steering wheel counterclockwise, not all the way just a little bit. Keep your right hand over your left, like this," she said and motioned.

I raised my right hand over the left while on the wheel and the car started turning. *I should not be doing this. I should not be doing this.*

"Okay, okay good, now start bringing your hands and the wheel back to the straight position so the car straightens out. Then we can just go straight for like a mile."

"Okay," I said. My throat felt dry. My heart was pounding like a drum. I really wanted to make it to my 14th birthday.

I couldn't fully get the coordination of things and my nerves were only making things worse. When I started to really think about what it was that I was doing, I would put too much pressure on the gas and go too fast and then freak out and switch to the brake too hard and jolt a little forward. I really didn't think I was passing this test.

"Okay, you're not going to make this light so be prepared to stop."

I started to wean my foot off of the gas pedal and steadily bring it back upright, ready to switch to the other. Brake.

"Don't panic, but there's a cop next to us at this light. Just look normal," Asher said.

Was she serious? Oh. My. God. There was truly a cop, a mean looking cop, right next to us. As in, the car sitting at the light in the lane next to us. This wasn't good. My pulse quickened. My throat closed more than it was before. I needed water.

"The light's green. Just go slow. But not too slow or he'll think we're drunk."

I froze. I couldn't move. I couldn't remember what to do. What pedal was what?

"Right pedal, slow," Asher encouraged. "Just trust me. Trust MASCARA."

My brain came back on and applied some light pressure to the gas. We were moving. The policeman turned on his blinker to turn. Thank God.

"Make this last turn and you can pull over, we're right by school."

I slowed down.

"Hit the blinker first."

I didn't transition well between moves but I got the job done. One right turn, a little stop and go, and I pulled over and brought the car to a stop. Asher pushed a triangular button and clicked her seatbelt open.

"Nice job. Task one complete. Now let's go have fun."

I was a little shaky as I began to get out of the driver's seat but I also felt really alive. Like, *really* alive. I couldn't wait to go the game having passed my first task and really, I just drove a car for the first time.

The overwhelming boom of the football game went through my whole body immediately. Asher and I had been stopped like 17 times from the parking lot to the entrance for the field. There were hordes of people, tons of different noises all melding together and this feeling of hometown.

There were Knights shirts and jackets everywhere and people with black and gold face paint. The thud of the marching band, the synchronized cheerleaders in short rhythmic chants, the energy and the weather.

I followed Asher as she walked behind the bleachers and typed a hundred miles an hour on her phone. Despite feeling a little self conscious about my outfit, and my hair, and my pimple (boy, this list was getting longer), I was so high on having driven Asher's car, I didn't seem to care. Everything else seemed to melt away. It was the same feeling I had when Derek changed my entire mood on a dime at the pep rally.

Speaking of Derek Mackey, was he here? Of course he was here, but where? Now that I was so deep into pledging MASCARA, I wasn't sure I even wanted to entertain this Derek thing. I mean Asher said he was off limits. Why was I even torturing myself? I had to cut it off plain and simple.

Mara walked up with two of the girls who were pledging, Ashley and Missy.

They too looked like they had just snorted rainbows and pure happiness.

"They passed," Mara said as she walked up to Asher.

"Good, because Carmen just text me that Megan Welsh didn't. She totally buckled and walked home."

Mara laughed. A little bit of an evil laugh if you ask me.

"Can't hack it, there's the door," she said. To who, I don't know, but she said it.

"It's not funny Mara. We're down to four girls and it's only week two. Do you have any idea how bad that is?"

Mara winced. "We only need two."

Asher shot Mara this look, a look that I'm not totally sure what it meant but I knew it meant something.

Carmen appeared out of thin air with Andy Flynn and things went silent.

"Yep, Megan bailed. Like a damn jailbird who just got pardoned. Not for nothing but my sister would've lasted ten times longer. These girls are weak," Carmen said. Then she turned to us, "No offense."

I was too happy to really care about what was going on. The reality was I was only up against one girl now and that was Missy Warwick. I wasn't going to lie to myself and think that Missy wasn't cute, because she was. She had this crimped hair that you couldn't make an iron do if you tried. It was just naturally amazing. And long. Okay yes, she had gorgeous hair. Before I knew it, I realized I was point blank staring at Missy. She looked at me and smiled. Damn, she had a killer smile too.

She knew she was up against me and only me. With my acne-riddled forehead and random hair and semi-cool clothes, she probably thought she had this in the bag.

I zoned out for a second too long and pictured Missy and I in one of those Western gun draws. Where I walk into a saloon and everyone stops what they're doing because I'm supposed to have a shootout to the death today with the one they call "Warwick." I'm chewing my toothpick and my thumbs are in my belt loops and I slowly walk through the bar and tip my hat. Warwick's outside waiting by her horse.

"Jorie, are you listening?"

Damn it.

"Yes," I said.

"Let's go grab some hot chocolate and get ourselves some seats," Asher said.

She seemed pissed. Why exactly, I didn't know.

"All of you, come with me," she said.

Missy, Andy and Ashley assembled a little behind me.

We walked to the concession stands. Every high schooler managed to turn their heads along the way. It was preposterous and exhilarating.

I turned to the other girls. "Did you guys drive?"

Ashley nodded.

"Yes!" Missy said, clearly excited.

"I've driven before," said Andy. "You guys haven't?"

She was a little condescending and seriously ruining my moment.

"No," I said.

"Your hair looks really cool, did you dye it or something?" Missy asked.

Damn it. I was beginning to like this girl. She was friendly. That wasn't good. How was I supposed to pull my big Western gun on her if she was friendly?

"Thanks," I said simply.

"What kind of car does Asher have?" Ashley asked me.

"A Mini Cooper," I answered. The girls clearly all were dying to know.

"What about Mara and Carmen?" I asked.

"Mara drives a really nice Lexus," Ashley said.

"Oh right, I think I knew that," I said.

"Carmen drives a convertible Mustang. We even put the top down," said Andy.

Woo hoo for you, I thought.

"Five hot chocolates," I heard Asher say to the concession lady.

"Did you hear that Rachel's parents bought her a Range Rover?" Ashley whispered.

"Really?" Missy said.

"Yep."

"Why did Megan bail?" I asked bluntly.

"Chickened out. Said she couldn't drive the car and didn't want to get arrested. Took her seatbelt off an' left," Andy said.

"Girls," Asher interrupted. She began to disperse piping hot chocolates.

"Thanks," I said and took a cup.

"Let's go under the bleachers so I can pour you guys some Bailey's in those. Hot chocolate isn't hot chocolate without a little Bailey's."

She motioned.

I didn't want to be the one to ask but I had absolutely no clue what Bailey's was.

"Bailey's sounds so good," I said anyway.

I did know that it was starting to get chilly and the hot chocolate in the Styrofoam felt good on my hands.

Ashley looked at me and whispered, "What's Bailey's?"

I tried my best not to laugh. I wanted to shrug but I couldn't.

Instead, we all followed.

That's when I saw Abby in the bleachers, looking like I skinned her cat.

More bad friend points.

I knew I was supposed to fight for her honor here. The truth was, I wasn't even sure if I liked Mara and Amanda was no picnic yet either. But I was still buzzing from driving Asher's car and I was in way too deep to drop the program. I mean I now had a 50/50 shot of getting in. All I had to do was be mindful of what Abby told me. Maybe I could help the situation, convince them to be cool to her.

We all ducked under a bleacher row one by one.

Asher pulled a roundish bottle from her bag.

"Okay give me your cups," she said.

Then I heard his voice.

"Miss Sutherland is that you boozing on school property again?" Derek said, mimicking a deeper voice.

"Piss off Mackey, I'm working," Asher said.

Derek lunged under the bleacher, suspending his arm but gluing his body to the ground.

I looked up and met his eyes. Damn it.

I extended my cup to Asher, eager to impress. Which of them, I'm not sure.

"Is that what you call it now, working?" Derek said and laughed.

The other pledges were ogling him. I guess so was I, but that was different. Right?

Another cute boy walked up behind Derek.

"Mackey stop harassing MASCARA girls. You're around them so much we're gonna paint your eyes blue soon," he said and playfully hit Derek's stomach.

Now I was thinking about Derek's stomach.

He looked so good in normal clothes. He had a baseball cap on. I had never seen him in a baseball cap. My God he looked cute. He should wear baseball caps everyday for the rest of his life.

I slurped my hot chocolate. I had to admit it tasted a lot better with Bailey's. I wasn't sure if I was going to get drunk or not. I got tipsy pretty easily so it was possible, but most likely a colossally bad idea.

"Everyone knows where they're sleeping tonight right," Asher asked the girls.

She blatantly ignored Derek and his friend. They took the hint and left.

How does she do that?

We all nodded.

"Good. We all have a lot of material to cover with you so make sure you meet back here as soon as the game ends. Go have fun," said Asher.

Where was I supposed to go now? It hadn't really dawned on me until now that I had been so attached to Asher, I didn't really know anyone else. Besides Abby, who definitely did not want to see me. I decided I should try anyway.

I walked to the bleacher where I passed Abby earlier. She was still there, this time with Bus Stop Boy.

"Hey Abby," I said.

"Hey."

I kicked the ground. I sipped my hot chocolate. I looked back at the start of the game. I watched Sue twirl around on the sidelines. This was awkward.

"Did you dye your hair?" she finally asked.

"Yea," I admitted. "Kind of."

"Hmm," she said. Which was obviously not a compliment in any way.

"Want some hot chocolate? There's Bailey's in it," I said and extended my cup.

"No way," Bus Stop Boy said. "Really?"

Abby shot him a death look. I guess he wasn't allowed to like me.

"Okay well, just wanted to say hi. I'll be around," I said.

I gulped the rest of the hot chocolate in one long gulp, which was hot on my throat and kind of hurt going down.

I wandered by myself through crowds of people and pops of noise. I didn't even care about the game, I was so distracted by everything. I also wasn't about to go sit by myself. My stomach was growling so I ventured off for French fries.

"Jorie!"

I turned.

Derek. Baseball cap wearin' Derek Mackey. In plain clothes. With a stomach I was still thinking about.

Everyone has a stomach Jorie. Stop.

"Oh hey," I said, maybe kind of coolly.

"Asher getting' you guys drunk?" he laughed. My God his teeth were so perfect. Perfect teeth. Teeeeth.

"We had some Bailey's," I said, still unsure of what that even meant.

"Ah Bailey's aint gonna getcha drunk. Come on now. You look way tougher than that," he said. He laughed. Then he kind of hit my arm. I felt a surge of something wonderful. That's all this boy had to do was graze my elbow and I felt like silly putty.

"Like what?"

"Have a real man's drink. Like whiskey!" he said.

"Oh yeah, you have a bartender around here?" I joked.

God I hope that was funny.

He laughed. I was entirely too happy that he laughed.

"You're cute," he said. Just like that.

I felt my face getting hot even though the rest of my body was starting to shiver.

"I'm not really a whiskey drinker," I said. I refused to look him in the eyes. I also refused to tilt my head down to give him better access to my pimple friend.

"Too classy? You must be a MASCARA then."

He didn't say this with fondness. I knew it was condescending. Not to me but to them.

"I'd drink a beer if you had one," I said trying to regain my un-classy Tomboy girl self. I also assumed he didn't have one.

I assumed wrong.

"Come on back by the guys. We have a cooler stashed," he motioned.

There was zero way out of this one. I started to walk.

"Derek!"

It was Adrianna and Amanda.

I'm screwed.

"What's my devilish brother up to now?" Adrianna asked.

"Big Macs looks like he's flirting to me," Amanda said. Her hair was again half up and slightly poofed in the front. I had to assume this was a signature hairstyle of hers.

"Better not be," Adrianna said with a tisk tisk finger movement.

"Oh he wasn't, we weren't," I said sounding incredibly guilty.

"Right," Amanda said. As pretty as she was, she was not very pretty on the inside.

"Will you two relax?" Derek said.

"Pledge come with us," Amanda said. "We need to keep an eye on you."

Was she serious? I didn't appreciate being called "pledge" even if that's what I was. Then there was the Abby thing.

I don't know if it was the Bailey's talking, especially since I still didn't even know what Bailey's was, or if I was just insulted, but to my surprise I said, "No, I'm fine."

"Oh you are are you?" Amanda asked. Her face said I did something very wrong here.

Amanda pulled her phone out. For all I knew she was logging onto the MASCARA app and telling them to kick me out for flirting and now telling her no. "No" was definitely not a word any of these girls heard often.

Derek gave a brotherly look to Adrianna.

Adrianna tugged at Amanda's jacket. "They're fine, let's just go eat."

Amanda feverishly punched keys on her phone. At this point, I felt like I didn't care. She disrespected my friend and then tried to humiliate me in front of Derek Mackey. I mean, I had a name. And it wasn't "pledge."

CHAPTER 11

"It's All in the Lighting"

Not even three minutes after the pledge incident happened did Asher text me to meet her by the front entrance. I knew their app was for evil.

I was walking about two feet behind Derek and trying not to look like I was walking *with* him to get a beer. I was a little relieved that she texted, the last thing I needed was to get caught having a beer on school property. Or worse, having a beer with him on school property by anyone else in MASCARA.

"Hey Derek, I need to take a raincheck. Asher just text me to meet her," I said.

He turned to me.

He was beautiful.

"You're in trouble aren't you?"

"Probably."

"I don't want to get you in trouble. Go. We can have that beer at my party next week."

I envisioned myself throwing my arms around him and kissing his exceptional mouth. The entire stadium stood up and clapped. Sue led the cheerleading squad in a "Go Jorie and Derek" chant.

"Jorie?"

I snapped out of it. "Huh?"

"Are you coming to the party next weekend?"

"I think so. My birthday is Tuesday so I just need to make sure my mom didn't plan anything. Oh, and I work on the weekends too so..." I trailed off.

"Just come for an hour. You owe me a rain check," he walked off with a smile.

I could tell I was smiling but I had a feeling in the pit of my stomach that Asher wouldn't be smiling. I had to cut this off, whatever it was. I was tempting fate here. Which did I want more? To be in MASCARA or to date a guy like Derek Mackey? How did I even know he wanted to date me? I didn't. He didn't. All he was offering was a beer. This was pure crazy.

I started for the entrance to meet Asher. I saw Rachel and Carmen sitting in their expensive clothes and color coordinated winter garb. Who looks good in a jacket and gloves? Only them, I decided. They didn't see me they were so lost in their phones.

"Hey Jorie," said the Liam boy I met the other day.

"Hey," I called back. Liam is cutey cute. Am I drunk?

Only two weeks into the school year and I felt like I knew so many people. It honestly was a good feeling.

In middle school, I barely talked to more than six people. I minded my business. I got good grades. I didn't care much for accessories or hair dye or blue make-up or any make-up for that matter.

I spent most of my time with Abby, who now hated me. Or kind of hated me. It wasn't like I was taking their side. She was just making it incredibly difficult to communicate with her. I decided to text her before I met up with Asher.

If it makes you feel any better, Amanda was a bitch to me too. Don't take it personally.

Send.

I spotted Asher as soon as I looked up from my phone. No matter where she was, people just gathered around her. She was like a statue people just wanted to marvel at from all over the world.

"Marjorie!" she called and waved me on.

Why did she insist on calling me Marjorie?

I picked up the pace.

I noticed the look on a few of the older kids faces. The who-the-Hell-is-Marjorie-look.

Yes, it's me. The unfortunately named, unfortunately pimpled, unfortunately dyed "pledge" me. Here I am. Shoo.

"Will you excuse me," Asher said to two people I didn't know.

She met me halfway.

"Amanda isn't happy with you. What happened?"

I breathed. Long. Hard. Exaggerated.

"I don't really know what to say. She called me 'pledge' and it just kind of bothered me."

Asher didn't say anything for a minute, just nodded.

Was I going to be blackballed?

"Why don't we get out of here? Go to my house early. There will be plenty of football games," she said.

"Are you mad at me?" I couldn't help but ask.

I already felt heartbroken for letting her down.

"I don't know yet. I don't really know what happened. But there's still so much you need to know and it's so early on in the program. Typically, we don't have any drops by now. I don't know what's going on with your grade but I take that as a reflection on us. So, if we aren't grooming you guys right, then extra time at the sleepover will only help things."

Damn she was mature.

Every word out of her mouth made me aspire to be more like her. I knew it was unfair to think this, but Abby seemed like such a kid with the silent treatments and triangling me out of conversations.

"Okay," I said. "Do you need to say goodbye to everyone?"

She smiled.

"I always leave the party first. Make that a rule of thumb. Keep people wondering. Keep them wanting more of you."

I laughed.

"Let's go. I'm driving this time," she said.

"Thank God!"

If I ever thought I had seen a big house before, like mansion in a TV show style big, I hadn't seen anything until I saw the Sutherland house. It was like a big house swallowed a big house and then that big house got pregnant with a house baby and they all moved in together. We're talking gargantuan.

This certainly didn't hurt the odds of making a lowly freshman reeeeally want to be in MASCARA. Not like she owned the house or worked for the house or would even inherit the house – but it just didn't hurt.

We pulled up in one of those super-winding driveways that curve toward the front doors. The lawn was so manicured it looked fake.

"Wow," I said.

"Thanks. My Dad invented a few websites and apps and sold them and then invested money or something and yea."

"Yea."

I was feeling really inferior right now. Like I was two inches tall and homeless.

"Your house is beautiful too you know," Asher said.

"Not like this," I said and sort of snorted.

I grabbed my overnight bags out of the back of her car. I half-expected a butler to walk up and grab my bags.

"You wouldn't believe how lonely a big house can feel," Asher said.

I didn't say anything.

"My mom passed away when I was seven. My Dad and I didn't live here at the time. It was just us. We lived on Tall Oaks Drive. He started making tons of money and then married my stepmom who stomped her feet until he got this house. Then they had my brother Caleb and then came my sister Hannah."

"I'm sorry to hear about your mom," I offered.

"Thanks. I was young. I remember her really well though. She was lovely."

"Do you get along with your stepmom?"

"Let's put it this way, in her eyes, her only kids are Caleb and Hannah. She is just waiting for me to go to college and leave them to their happy family."

"That can't be true," I said.

"Oh it is. My Dad just makes up for it with credit cards."

Asher opened the front door.

I assumed this conversation was on hold.

Asher held her pointer finger to her lips.

"Kids are sleeping," she whispered.

I shut the door carefully.

The house was ten times as intimidating on the inside as it was on the outside. You could literally get lost in it. I wondered how many rooms were in this place but now was certainly not the time to ask.

"Come upstairs," Asher said quietly.

I toted my bags behind her up a spiral staircase. I immediately realized how odd it was not to be greeted when you walked in the house. No one was waiting up for her. I didn't know if I felt bad for her or jealous. She could get away with murder.

My mom was always pouncing on me as soon as I walked in the door. Speaking of which, I needed to text her.

We got to the top of the stairwell and walked down a hall that felt like the size of our school.

"Last room on the right," Asher said. "I'll be right in."

"Okay."

I reached the last door on the right, which appropriately read 'Asher' in big blue letters.

I walked in Asher's room and nearly threw up.

It was the size of half my house. Literally.

A huge canopy bed lie in the middle of the room, with swooping sheers and a million pillows – like a showroom bed. Sleek, modern dressers lined the outside – a slate grey, shiny. They housed at least twenty drawers, which I assumed were all clothes. A walk-in closet stood open and full of orderly hangers. I'd say eighty percent of the closet was blue. There was also a small section of just uniform variations. I could still see tags still hanging off most of the clothes. Clothes with labels. Shiny designer labels I didn't even know.

I switched on a lamp for a better look. She had a bathroom hanging off the side of her room, packed with more products than a store. The girl had a marble shower.

Along her dressers were tons of pictures, some framed some not. A Junior Prom Queen sash, dried flower petals, antique perfume bottles, poetry books, a delicate floral tea set, stacks of fashion magazines that looked like they were in order of month, unopened packages of the infamous cobalt mascara, autographs I couldn't quite make out the names behind and candles melted down to wax piles. Her room was, in one word, amazing.

I put my bag down and wandered into the bathroom. I so badly wanted to know what hair products she used even though I knew they'd be ridiculously out of my reach. I clicked on a light but still found the room to be somewhat dim.

"I have them set to school lighting," Asher said as she walked in.

"Excuse me?"

"The lights. I asked the janitor to tell me the lighting they used at school and had my Dad put them in. There's the gym lights, the hall lights, classroom lights, even school dance lights."

"You're lying, no way," I said.

"Seriously. It's easier for me to do my make-up and know what I'm actually going to look like at school if the lighting matches."

This was too much.

"Well, what good does it do me to get ready all morning in one light and then get to school and have it all look totally different?"

The girl had a point, but c'mon.

"Try it. The last one is school dance lighting," she urged.

I flipped the last switch upright.

Yep. Looked like a school dance alright, even though I hadn't yet seen one at Saint Lawrence. Our middle school dances were so lame. I was actually looking forward to a real dance.

"You were Prom Queen? That's so cool," I said, rather uncool-like.

"Sure. You can be too if you stick with MASCARA. Someone from MASCARA always wins," Asher said.

She started to grab a bunch of random items from her bathroom drawers while she talked.

"What made you want to join anyway?" I asked.

"What makes anyone want to join? Popularity? Power? Fun? Control?"

She handed me a bunch of beauty products.

"Here take these," she said.

There were cucumber eye masks and exfoliating peels and facial spin brushes and a ton of other things I had never cared to use.

"Come sit," she said.

I followed. Not because I was a pet Chihuahua but because I was genuinely intrigued.

She had a big shaggy rug in the center of the room near her bed. She spilled the things in her hands on the rug and then went to her sleek and modern slate colored TV stand that matched her incredible furniture.

I had oak furniture. Oak.

"Okay but was there, like, a you?"

She laughed. "What do you mean?"

She retrieved two blue wine glasses and a bottle of wine, blush in color.

I wasn't sure how to say what I meant. "Like, was there someone guiding you. A you to me, but for you."

"Oh. Of course! Michelle Chase. She was by far the coolest girl in school. In the world in my opinion. I still see her all the time. She goes to college with my boyfriend."

"You have a boyfriend?" I blurted out.

This threw my world off its axis. I always pictured Asher single. I don't know why, I just did.

"Why does that surprise you?"

"Oh I didn't mean it offensively. You just seem so independent."

"I am. Frankie and I are both very independent. And next year when we're both in college together, we'll still be that way."

"Did he go to Saint Lawrence?"

Asher smiled. "I need to go get us ice. Do you know how to use a wine opener?"

"Not unless you like the taste of cork," I said honestly.

"Okay, stay right here. I'll get ice."

"Sure."

I noticed she avoided the question of whether or not her boyfriend went to Saint Lawrence. The only question was why.

I remembered I wanted to text my mom that I was safe. I noticed a text from Abby:

Amanda is awful. Most of them are. I'm happy to see you agree.
I thought you were turning into one of them. LOL.

I couldn't write LOL back. It was a stupid rule but I wasn't in good graces tonight and I wanted to break the habit of cheesy acronyms.

I hear ya.

I didn't know what else to write. I hit send and hoped she didn't take it the wrong way. Some of the girls could be awful. Amanda was awful. I decided to text my mom and move on:

At Asher's. In for the night. Call if you need me.
I'll be at the store tomorrow morning.

I heard Asher clinking ice on her way back. I couldn't believe there were still no parents in sight.

"So. About Derek Mackey," she said.

She jammed a silver bottle opener into a cork and twisted and pulled like a pro.

It dawned on me that if I got drunk I was liable to say very stupid things about my crush on Derek. What if that was her mission? I panicked.

"There's nothing fun to talk about there. I'd so much rather hear about your college boyfriend than some stupid high school guy."

I could not believe my own ears. I had just manipulated a conversation. That was so highly unlike me.

Asher semi blushed. "You got that right. College guys and high school boys are worlds apart. And yes, Frankie went to Saint Lawrence. He wasn't a first and last name guy but I did meet him when I was pledging."

She poured me a glass over ice and handed it to me.

Drink slow Jorie. Baby sips.

I started to picture myself completely sloshed and telling her every stupid thing I had thought about Derek Mackey in a matter of hours. About his stomach. His lips. Us kissing while the entire stadium stood up and clapped.

I had to drink slow.

I sipped.

"So what, you waited until after you got in?"

"Yep."

Keep the conversation on Asher and Frankie.

I continued, "Let me see a picture!"

Asher sipped her wine. Well, chugged is a better word.

She giddily got up from the rug where I was sitting and ran to fetch pictures.

How was this happening? I was manipulating Asher Sutherland.

She flashed a picture in my face of her and a very cute guy, who looked like he was in college, in front of a roller coaster.

"He is so cute," I said.

"I know."

She showed me another. And another.

I sipped more wine. All I had to do was keep her on Frankie.

"So you've been together for like four years?" I asked.

"Almost."

I sipped some more.

"Wanna hear this new song Mara found. It's incredible."

"Sure," I said.

Asher fiddled with speaker wires.

"Great. Before we do that, let's talk about you and Derek."

Zing. She won. You can't out-manipulate a manipulator, apparently.

I had finished my wine. It wasn't so easy to play down the Derek thing now.

I felt a smile peeking through my very best straight face. I tried to stifle it. I even bit the inside of my mouth hoping to control it. I couldn't even manipulate my own mouth.

"Like I said, there's nothing to tell."

"Marjorie, it's written all over your face. Plus, Amanda posted it in the app tonight."

"I knew it," I mumbled.

"What?" she asked.

"Nothing."

"Look, I understand that Derek Mackey liking you is a big deal. I get it. I really do. But every guy at Saint Lawrence is going to like you right now. And I just think you can do better. Plus, rules are rules. You can't date while you're pledging."

I was quiet.

"We're just friends," I finally said. "We're not dating. No one's dating anyone."

"Okay," Asher said. "Good."

She put a song on that I'd never heard before. "This is Love Trumps Crush. Ever hear of them? They're playing here in like a week and we'll probably all go."

"Cool, I like 'em."

Asher poured more wine into my glass.

"What is all this stuff anyway?" I asked, fingering the collection of products she put on the rug.

"These are all from Rachel. She holds Beauty Chair. We've done a pretty lousy job of explaining the chairs to you guys but there's just been so much going on this week. Next week we can have a real meeting but tonight is what's known as first sleepover."

"First sleepover?"

"Yes. It's all really a big formula. First sleepover is between a member of MASCARA and the girl they picked to give a bid to. Which is why you're here."

I nodded and inspected some sort of face wash.

"In MASCARA, we have monthly meetings. Usually we go for mani/pedis or something and then we all go over upcoming trends and whatever news we have. So, Rachel will basically teach us what she's found in beauty lines, or what products to be using or if something was found to be unanimal friendly, etcetera," Asher explained.

"That sounds like a lot of work," I said honestly. It was the wine blabbing.

"It is a lot of work. No one said any of this was easy. Carmen has to stay on top of every fashion trend so far in advance. And she is so good at it. I don't know what MASCARA will do when she graduates."

"Well, that chair won't be mine I can assure you of that."

Stop drinking Jorie.

Asher smiled. "Carmen has an edge. Her mom is this big international buyer and always flies to Paris or Prague or Seoul so it's not like Carmen is just reading *Vogue* or something."

"No way, that's awesome," I said. I didn't even know two of those places.

Asher started squeezing a tube of something into her hands.

"Rachel had us switch to this soy based face cream last month. I don't notice a difference but she swears by it."

She rubbed some onto my hand. "Try it."

I usually just used soap and water and called it a night. I had so, so much to learn. It looked like Asher spent a solid hour prepping just to go to sleep.

I rubbed a circle of cream onto my cheek.

I started laughing. "I have no idea," I said.

"You're getting drunk," Asher laughed.

"Maybe I am."

"Okay well before you wind up passing out, I have a few more things you need to know."

I tuned in. As best as I could. I was just starting to sense a headache coming on. Oh no, was I getting my period? I didn't even know what day it was anymore. Oh right, three days before my birthday. Must be a wine headache.

"We have Dress Down Days at Saint Lawrence once a month. You'll wear my clothes. Get ready here. I'll help you."

"Check."

"There's a Halloween Dance coming up. You'll go with Liam Nelson."

"Wait. Uncheck. Why?"

"Because that's the way it is. You can't date but we can't have you show up alone to a dance. He's cute and he's a freshman. Go with Liam."

"Did you guys put him up to this?"

"Not really."

What was she saying? My God was everything in MASCARA calculated?

"Senior Slave Day is also next week," Asher went on.

"What does that even mean?"

"It means freshmen do anything that seniors say the entire school day and it can be extremely humiliating. Most of the seniors already know who you are personally and wouldn't dare trying. But Mara and I can't show favoritism so we will treat you as we would anyone else. Just know it's all in good fun and after the bad comes the good."

"What does that mean?"

"It means that afterwards, because of us, you four pledges get to go to a Macs party which is so worth it. And no other freshman go but MASCARA pledges."

She continued, "Senior Slave Day was planned this year so that it falls on Dress Down Day. I think the seniors all got shirts made that say 'SENIORS' on them and wanted to wear them. It's not a good thing though because they can make you do way more in jeans than they can in a uniform."

Asher was lining her teeth with some kind of whitening strip and started talking kind of lispy.

"Lastly, and you won't know when, you have another task coming up. Some time next week is all I can tell you so stay on your toes," she said "toes" like "toth" to which I did my best not to laugh.

Asher's phone rang.

She answered it and started talking cryptically while I searched around for mine. I had a text from Abby:

I'm so happy to hear you say that.

And also my mom:

Be careful and we'll see you tomorrow.

Asher hung up her phone.

"Mara's outside with Amanda. I'll be right back. Stay here."

Outside? Now? I was jealous of how much of a family they all felt like. No one ever showed up at my house at midnight. I seriously just wanted to move into Asher's house and hijack her existence.

"Okay sure," I said.

Something hit the window. Not hard but enough to make me jump a little.

Asher rolled her eyes and walked over to the window. She lifted it open.

"Hey kitten! Get down here!" I heard two giggly and definitely drunk girls say.

"Coming gypsies!" she called back to them.

"Amanda's all pissy with you so just hang tight," she said to me.

"Okay," I nodded. My lids felt heavy.

Within minutes, I was asleep. On the shaggy rug.

CHAPTER 12

"Banish the Teddy Bears"

"Marjorie. Marjorie wake up."

Someone was shaking me. I opened one eye. I felt thirsty. I opened my other eye.

"You should make it a habit to never fall asleep with make-up on," Asher said staring at me.

My neck hurt. My head hurt. My hurt hurt if a hurt could hurt.

"Ugh," I managed to get out.

"I made you a smoothie. It has three superfoods in it. It's good for you, drink it."

I propped up on an elbow and took the thick green concoction.

"What happened?"

"You passed out. I came back upstairs after Mara and Amanda came by and you were in twilight."

How embarrassing.

"Oh." I knew I probably looked like a mess. Asher, on the other hand, looked like, well, Asher.

"You can use my shower. Drink the smoothie, it has green tea to give you energy. Use Vaseline to get all that make-up off and in general, use it every night, it'll keep underneath your eyes smooth and supple. I'll drive you to work on my way to yoga."

Is there anything this girl can't do? Was she saving cats from trees and then making rhubarb pie this afternoon? My God, she was like a Pinterest board in a human being.

"Okay." I pulled my lazy non-yoga non-Soul Cycle non-superfood (what's a superfood?) body up and managed to walk to the bathroom. I passed all sorts of MASCARA propaganda along the way. It really did look like she had four amazing years in high school. Well, three and change.

Onto stalking her hair products...

I wound up five minutes late to work and my dad didn't let me live it down the entire day. He acted like five minutes without me at Carr Water Shop was going to shut down the water supply to the entire country, when in reality, five minutes made no difference to anyone anywhere.

There were five Carr Water Shops in the US. My dad was scouting a sixth location. We sold filter systems for houses, offices, schools, what have you, plus coolers, and then trinkets about hydration or teeny desk fountains or sports bottles. If it had to do with water, we basically sold it.

I helped out on the weekends despite the fact that we *had* employees and those employees made much more money than I did. My parents wanted me to get used to a job. Understand responsibility.

The only thing I understood so far was that I had sacrificed practically all of my weekends for a year already.

On a positive note, we also helped raise money for good water-friendly causes like building wells in Africa. From time to time my Dad had to travel to all sorts of places I had never heard of or couldn't pronounce.

My mom helped at the store once in a while but most of the time she stayed at home with Matt and took care of "the books" which I think meant the financial stuff.

I was fighting to keep my eyes open by the time my shift ended and my mom and Matt came to pick me up.

"Abby came by earlier today," my mom said as I clicked together my seatbelt.

"She did? Why?"

"She looked very upset Marjorie. Said something about girls not liking her at school," my mom said with an open-ended look on her face like question marks were about to rise from her head.

"What time was that?" I asked.

"Probably about noon," my mom said, still waiting for me to volunteer information.

Why would Abby come by the house on a Saturday afternoon? She knows I work Saturdays, every single Saturday. Why wouldn't she have called or come down to the store?

My mom was fishing for something she could tell Abby's mom and I wasn't about to give it to her.

I had to do something. I had to sort this out with Abby. Because as the seconds ticked by, our friendship was dying a slow death.

I hadn't really realized it until I came home that night that I had the night off from MASCARA. And I didn't know the first thing to do with myself. I tried calling Abby twice but she didn't pick up.

I began to pace around my room and the more I paced, the more I realized how childish it was. The room, not the pacing. I had these nets in each ceiling corner holding stuffed animals.

Stuffed. Animals.

Some were from carnivals, the really crappy kind that you win despite not actually doing the one thing you had to do to win, like pop a balloon. There's always a row on the bottom at those carnival games that shelve something closer to dog toys but the poor guy that's trying to rile up the crowd (that usually ignores him) says "You getta prize no matter what!"

I never did switch two of those small prizes for a medium prize so voila! I have full caddy-cornered nets filled with really ghetto stuffed animals. About a handful were from when I broke my ankle in third grade. Bears with crutches and bandages or whatever.

I thought about Asher's room and how incredibly grown up it was. All of the creams and masks and candles and poems and sleek furniture and stashed wine bottles. She had wine bottles, I had teddy bears.

I started to pick them off one by one and stuff them into a plastic storage bin. I also tried not to look at my phone. I really genuinely wanted Abby to call me back so I could untangle her whole mess. I also somewhere secretly wanted my phone to just ring. I wanted people to call me like they did Asher. I wanted people to show up at my house and make it feel less alone. I wanted Derek to have gotten my number from Adrianna and text me something amazing.

However...

My phone was as quiet as my dead teddy bears stuffed in a bin. I shut the ringer off so that I wouldn't know that no one was calling me. This way when people did call and text, I would be too "busy" to answer. And if no one did? Well, then I won't know that during every painstakingly quiet moment.

Ten minutes later when I checked it anyway, not one single thing had happened.

I started peeling every single item out of my closet and building a burn pile. I wasn't literally going to burn them. At least I didn't think I was. I just had to never see them again staring back at me from my wardrobe. Bleagh.

My burn pile was about ten times the size of my keep pile. I had practically no clothes I liked, which was a bonus for private school. I was actually feeling quite thankful to God that I had uniforms.

I was also feeling quite thankful that Asher didn't come upstairs and see my bedroom when she was here.

I was back in my Queen Asher and King Derek vision form the pep rally – where the King tells me to banish the teddy bears and the Queen scoffs at my "pauper's threads" that I call clothes – when my mom rapped on my door.

"Marjorie, Abby is at the door. She looks like she's been crying."

CHAPTER 13

"Acclimation"

On Tuesday morning, which just so happened to be my birthday, I started thinking about one of my vocabulary words, "acclimation." It's kind of like adaptation. The dictionary says: "It usually means getting accustomed to a particular new climate, but it can also mean getting used to other situations, such as a new school."

The thing about acclimation is that we can also acclimate to environments or situations that are horrific. Think about a sick relative or a car accident... At first, it's "Oh my God!-bad" but after you just sort of let the bad soak in, once it finally bleeds back out, it's more like "Eh, I'm used to it." Not so bad.

So, I'm now fourteen and applying my English Lit vocabulary word to my body's getting used to being treated like a pledge.

Do this, get that, come here.

I still hadn't said anything to anyone in MASCARA about Abby. I started to, like three times, but then it ended more with them giving me some sort of order than me asking any questions.

Me: "Do you know a—"

Anyone in MASCARA: "Can you get me a water from the vending machine?"

Abby told me Saturday that she thought they all hated her and that they were making her life a living Hell. She said she wanted to transfer to Willow Grove. What could they possibly be saying to her to make her want to switch schools? I knew I had to intervene and I would. I just needed a plan.

There was a big smiley face sticker stuck to my locker. I didn't know where it came from but it made me laugh. I noticed Abby out of the corner of my eye with Bus Stop Boy, whose name was actually Jake.

Abby told me Saturday night that she was certain that one of the MASCARA girls must have a thing for Jake and that's why they're being so mean to her and making her cry. I couldn't see how that was possible. They were out of his league. They could get guys that Abby just couldn't. Nevertheless.

I opened my smiley-faced adorned locker to find two blue cards.

One looked like a regularly-scheduled MASCARA card and the other quite possibly a birthday card.

"Happy Birthday," I heard from somewhere behind me.

I turned to see the back of Derek Mackey walking toward the senior hallway. How did he manage to make something I've heard ten times today sound utterly and completely different than the way everyone else had said it?

He didn't stop, just smiled.

That's when it hit me. The sticker had to be from him. I just knew it. If it was from anybody else I'm sure I would've thought it was stupid. Childish, even. From Derek? Ridiculously amazing. How did he do that? Another guy could pull a sword from a stone right in front of me right now, all in my honor of course, and I would think Derek's little puddle of effort was better.

Sigh. (The action not the store.)

I opened the first card:

Happy Birthday Jorie!
Always,
MASCARA

I opened the second.

Marjorie,

We found out that Mr. Mayer has an online dating profile. Your task is to create a fake profile and use it to flirt with him. We're having all of you girls make one so you will have some competition for his heart! Be creative and let us know your screen name as soon as you create one. If you need to be eighteen, use my birthday. It's on your contact sheet.

Always,
Asher
P.S. – He's on Matcher!

An online dating site prank on a teacher? This doesn't sound like it ends well. Was it legal to semi-cyberstalk your teacher? Was it legal to give someone pledging errands on their own birthday?

Like I was saying… Acclimation.

I have acclimated to this new planet where Abby kind of hates me and might transfer. Abby also has a boyfriend. I can't have a boyfriend but I'm told who to go to a dance with and cards are dictating my life, all in the pursuit of a mascara.

The acclimation part? That I don't even question this crazy planet I'm on anymore, I just nod in zombaic (there's that word again) contentment and obey.

I did need a plan when it came to Abby. A way to find out why they were bullying her and put a stop to it. If I do get in, then I would have a say. They would like whoever I liked. Wouldn't they? But if I got blackballed, she would continue to get bullied for the rest of her high school career.

Then it dawned on me. I might too. So being blackballed helped no one here. Hence, I have to keep acclimating to this dough-like thing I have become.

As I raced to class, I decided right then and there what my mission had to be. To take out Missy Warwick and leave no option but for me to get in. I had to flirt and flirt like hell with Mr. Mayer, I had to pass this task with flying colors and make things right.

"Hey Jorie, Happy Birthday," Liam said as he passed.

"Thanks," I said and smiled, somewhat genuinely. How did he know it was my birthday? Did he also know he was sentenced by the Queen to go to the Halloween Dance with me? Had he acclimated as well? Were we all just robots? Despite how very late I was running, I stood there in the hallway for a moment and pictured everyone as robot – their heads square and metal, their bodies slow and mechanical and robot-sounding.

DZZZZPPPT.

I finally breezed into my class just as the bell was ringing. That was as close to on time as I got these days.

Mr. Walsh did this kind of head shake nod thing when I walked in. The "I'm disappointed, you could have been a much better student if you cared more" look. I hated that look. He had basically acclimated to my being a thorn in his side and I am starting to acclimate to his frowny face.

Age: 37
Hair Color: Blonde
Eye Color: Green
Body Type: Slim/Slender
Profession: Veterinarian
Drink: Socially

Smoke: Never
Marital Status: Divorced

I was up to the "About Me" section of my, sorry I mean "LuLuForYou's," profile on Matcher when I kind of got stumped. I was hunched over my phone in lunch and building "Lulu's" page out to things I assumed Mr. Mayer liked but really what did I know what he liked? Physical Education.

He liked being physical. Lulu can be physical.

This was not the way I pictured my birthday, pretending to be a girl named Lulu and flirting with a teacher – an unattractive teacher at that.

I needed to look through fake photos at some point and find an actual Lulu. I knew I could do this when I got home but I didn't want to get caught by my mom and I didn't want the other pledges to have more time with their fake profiles and get a head start on Mr. Mayer.

"This seat taken?" I heard and immediately jumped. I slid my sweater sleeve over my phone screen. It was Liam.

"You're everywhere aren't you?"

"Girl shouldn't be sitting at lunch alone on her birthday," he said. He slid a tray next to me.

I hadn't really let myself realize it before, but he was quite good looking in a sporty-I'm-sure-everyone-noticed-but-me kind of way. He had a squarish jaw like a rich cartoon character that drives a fancy cartoon car and carries bags with actual dollar signs on it. He didn't seem like a freshman. He seemed mature, like he grew up with a lot of rules. Like where to put his shoes when he walked in the door.

"It's no biggie, I was working on something anyway," I said.

"Jorie. Look, my sister Aimee is six years older than I am."

"That's great," I said, entirely unaware of where he was going with this.

"She was a MASCARA. I know how it works, how it all works basically. They're completely formulaic so that traditions are preserved so very little changes. Anyway, I know you have to go to the Halloween Dance with me," he said.

I could swear my eyes were actually bugging out of their sockets, still connected to vessels but just veiny balls straight popping forward.

"Seriously?"

"Seriously. Alumni can get on the app and Aimee was on the other night chatting or whatever it is they do on there. I'm totally fine with it. I think we'll have fun."

I didn't want to look at all discouraged because Liam seemed like a really, really nice guy. Unfortunately, Derek Mackey's face was running through my head and I secretly wished I was allowed (allowed?) to go somewhere with him.

I had acclimated to being allowed or not allowed by a group of girls I had known under a month. Liam had, flashback to the robots, acclimated apparently as well. To what a group of girls tell his sister on an app they basically created.

I drank a sip of my soda and thought about what this meant. Then, it all came spilling out: "What did Aimee tell you about Senior Slave Day? Do you know what the tasks are? What else is on the app? What does Aimee do now, like for a living? What's her boyfriend like? Does she have one?"

"Whoa, whoa, hold on, hold on. One at a time, killer. And first you answer my question."

I laughed. A real laugh. "What?"

"Wow, you're really pretty when you smile," Liam said. "Now are you going to this dance with me or what?"

This was when puzzle pretty revealed itself. All of a sudden he noticed he liked my smile even though he has probably found me rather blah until now. I'm okay with that.

"Sure," I said. "Now tell me about Aimee."

⁂

I cropped the photo of fake Lulu to fit the profile square as soon as I got on the bus home. Asher text me during ninth period and told me that Mr. Mayer was showing an interest in "Fawn," which was Andy Flynn's fake girl.

I couldn't let Mr. Mayer like Andy's fake girl over my fake girl. Obviously. So my fake girl had to be leaps and bounds above her fake girl. Was I seriously thinking these things? Again, I reminded myself – acclimation is key...

So there I was, bum-rushing the bus after school and searching Lulus like they were going out of style. Once I decided on wild blond Veterinary Assistant Lulu over calm brunette nurse Lulu, I typed the world's most charming "About Me" section, just enough quirks to be believable but damn was she loveable. I sort of wanted to date her myself.

Then I hit Mr. Mayer with my first "flirt."

"Hi Handsome."

That's all I wrote. Because it was kind of perfect. It was forward. It was conservative. It was mysterious. It left him wanting more. It left the door open for potential crazy since, let's be honest, Mr. Mayer was anything but handsome. It was open-ended. It neatly kicked a ball in his court. It was short and non-narcissistic. It was perfect. Then I waited. Biting my nails, I waited by pretending I wasn't waiting.

And I thought about Liam's sister Aimee that I didn't even know. And I wondered what I could find out from him. And I wondered if alumni could help me get Abby in MASCARA's good graces. And I wondered if I even wanted Abby in MASCARA's good graces. And I wondered where Derek was right at this moment and why Asher was so Hell bent on us not dating. And I wondered what I had to do on Senior Slave Day and what fabulous clothes I would be dressed in. And I wondered about the Halloween Dance. And I wondered about life in general a little bit because c'mon how could I not? Everything was so chaotic.

When I got to my house, I walked into the awkward surprise party of the century. My mom, Abby's mom, Abby, and my brother Matt stood around a melty ice cream cake and one or two hopeful balloons. There were a few neatly wrapped boxes and a frayed Happy Birthday banner taped to the cabinets. I'd barely even said three words to Abby in weeks and I was pretty certain her mom had forced this on her.

"Happy Birthday Jorie," Abby said.

Mrs. Port followed suit. "The big one-four," she said.

I was preoccupied with fake Lulu. I was trying to listen for my phone to ding and indicate a message from Matcher.

My mom had just lit her last match and now everyone was singing in tone-deaf-unison. "Happy Birthday to you..."

CHAPTER 14

"Lulu's Last Laugh"

I'm embarrassed to say I stayed up all night flirting with gross Mr. Mayer. I had no idea how I was going to face him in gym class today.

Let me back up. I absent-mindedly faked my way through the awkward birthday party. Abby made two, not one but two, comments about my "new life" and my "new friends" in front of our collective moms which was making it increasingly harder to feel bad for her.

She bought me an expensive make-up kit, which when I tore open the wrapping paper, she said, "The mascara is black, not like your new friends wear."

My mom had seen my cobalt eyes but still knew very little of what was going on. I didn't know what Mrs. Port knew. All I knew was that the gift was an insult.

"Thanks," I said and beamed a wide smile.

My mom had bought me some clothes I would never wear and also gave me two gift cards. One to *Sigh*, for which I was grateful. My Dad would later bring me home a teddy bear because unbeknownst to him, the teddy bears had left the net.

After the cake and poor singing and bear collector faking, Abby and I had gone to my room.

"I'm working on a plan you know," I said, while hanging up my new clothes I'd never wear.

"For what?" Abby asked me like I was talking about some covert thing she'd never heard of. Like she didn't have a clue in the world as to what I could be referring to.

"For what? My CIA operation, what do you mean for what? For you. With MASCARA."

Abby was eyeing up my room.

"I don't want you to work out a plan. Those girls are so mean, I want nothing to do with them. Where are all your bears?"

I was a little dumbfounded. "They obviously just don't know you. And if I get in, I can change all that. But if I don't get in, then I can't help anything."

"What I don't understand, is why you'd want to get in at all. I mean, Jor, I've told you for weeks that they're torturing me and you still want to be a part of something like that."

I didn't know what to say. Was she right? Should I drop? Was I so acclimated that I didn't realize that these were evil people? Evil to my one and only friend that I had at Saint Lawrence.

"What would you do if you were in my shoes Ab?"

Abby looked like she was going to cry. I felt like someone just stabbed me.

She didn't say a word.

"Should I drop out?"

Abby fingered a picture of us that was on my mirror. Like she was questioning whether she'd ever be in my room again.

"I don't know what you should do. I can't tell you what to do," she finally said.

"It's not like your friends like me. Your new guy and your new BFF," I said, sounding way more bitter than I actually felt.

"They're just being protective," Abby said.

I thought about this for a second. Why was it okay for her friends to be protective, but not mine?

"What if the girls in MASCARA are just being protective of me?"

"It's not the same," she said.

"Why not?"

"It's just not. Do whatever you want. I have to get home. Happy Birthday," she said, and let herself out.

I didn't know where to take out my emotions so I took to Lulu. Probably not the brightest idea I had ever had but at the time it felt right.

Mr. Mayer had written back, "Great pic" to my "Hi Handsome."

I didn't know in that moment what I was going to do about pledging, but I did feel like I needed a good distraction from everything. This was what sparked a four-hour conversation with my gross teacher.

The worst part? He seemed like a genuinely nice guy. A nice, lonely guy. One who thought that maybe this super attractive blond woman was interested in him.

But, those feelings didn't hit me last night. They hit me today.

It was Wednesday morning, the day before Senior Slave Day/Dress Down Day and I was sitting in homeroom feeling like fourteen was already the most confusing year of my life. Okay, that's a bit dramatic. But I was upsetting my best friend and dangling fake carrots to nice gym teachers. What was next? Rip off a baby? Skin a puppy? Sock my grandma in the stomach?

Anders Cavelli looked fresh and happy in the back of homeroom. She was back to good ole regular black mascara and no rules. She could date whom she wanted and enjoy her birthday and leave gym teachers alone.

For the first time, I felt jealous of the girl who dropped out. When the bell rang, I sort of poured out of my desk like slow moving sludge, un-anxious to go through the rest of this day and it had just started. How on Earth was I going to get through tomorrow?

"How's pledging going?" I heard.

I looked up and saw Anders.

"Not bad," I lied.

"Good for you. Stay strong," she said.

What an odd thing to say. Was I headed to war?

She walked off, still looking so damn happy. And free.

I went to my locker. Abby wasn't at hers. I didn't know if she took the bus because my mom drove me this morning after I fashionably missed it. It is virtually impossible to make yourself look decent every day when you had to wear the same clothes.

Just as I thought this, Rachel Whitley and Mara French walked passed my locker, looking impeccably perfect. That shoots that theory to Hell.

"You ready for tomorrow pledgling?" Mara called.

I couldn't even tell if she was being mean or this was just her personality anymore. I think she fully thought she was being nice.

"Of course," I said back.

They marched toward the senior hallway arm-in-arm and literally there were at least five freshmen staring at me, all because Mara and Rachel spoke to me. It didn't even matter if Mara was being mean, I was still the unicorn urban legends were made of – the freshman that seniors talked to.

I felt like people wanted to pet me and see if I was real. As creepy and somewhat carney freakshow-ish as it felt, it also felt really mortifyingly exhilarating.

Imagine if I was arm-in-arm with Mara French? Imagine if by the end of this school year I knew all the fashion dirt and the soy-based face washes in the world? Imagine if I skipped through the freshmen hallway as a bona fide member of MASCARA? Too good to be true.

And just like that, that one weak moment and inhalation of popularity crack, and I forgot all about how bad of a human I was. Mr. Mayer just disintegrated into a pile of "whoops." And Abby was a shoulder shrug.

In my locker was a blue card, which I had become really accustomed to and kind of looked forward to getting.

Marjorie,

Tonight all four of you guys need to ask Mr. Mayer on a date. Hopefully you can all ask right after school. Whoever he actually agrees to meet, will get a pass on a future task. Be charming! I have to give you clothes for tomorrow so I will drive you home today. Meet me in the parking lot.

Always,
Asher

Back to reality. This poor guy was going to get stood up tonight. Now *that*, seemed cruel. It was one thing to cyber-prank but taking it to real life was low. Ugh.

I folded the card back up and dug out my history book. Which should have been home with me because I should have been working on a report that I had five days to finish and I hadn't even started. Slacker.

I had like two minutes to make it to class when—

"There you are kid. Did you ever get my sticker on your locker? It was a birthday gift."

I didn't even have to look up to know who it was.

The sight of him made my knees weaken. As in, literally not like a southern romance novel – I could barely stand straight.

"What up D. Macs," some kid said as he walked by.

Derek nodded to the boy but kept his focus on me. Me.

I was becoming aware I hadn't said anything yet.

"That was you? I had no idea," I said like I didn't care.

"Really? I thought for sure you'd know it was me," he said. I wanted to bite his eyes. Not in a vampire kind of way, but in the way you want to bite a cute small animal. They were so puppy-ish and captivating. His stare was so intense.

"Thank you, it was cute," I said.

"Will I see you at my house Friday?"

Let's be honest. If Derek Mackey asked me to go to the Bermuda Triangle with him I would go, so this was a no-brainer.

"Maybe," I said instead. I smiled a confident and flirty smile at him. Maybe it was all the practice I had gotten with Mr. Mayer. Suddenly, I was the flirting champion of the world.

"Are you playing hard to get Ms. Jorie Carr?" he asked.

Wow. Was it ever weird to hear him say my full name. I mean, I said his full name all the time but that's because he was Derek Mackey.

Was I becoming a first name last name-r? A heartbreaking mouthful on someone's lips? Ms. Jorie Carr. Did he call me Jorie Carr in his head? No way, too surreal.

"Not at all. Maybe I will be at the party, maybe I won't," I taunted.

Adrianna came bounding up behind him and half-jumped on his back. "How's my favorite brother?"

Derek broke his gaze. "Save it Adge, we all know Rob is your favorite."

"False," she said.

I couldn't imagine how fun their house must be. To have three siblings so close in age, all in high school together. It's like you always had friends over. I was envious. Matt and I would never be in school together, we were just world's apart.

"I have to get to class, see you guys later," I said.

"Tell Mr. Mayer I said 'hi' Jorie," Adrianna called to me. A little too loudly for my liking.

Twinge.

There was that good ole' guilt I had become used to. I had all but forgotten I had to set up my gym teacher to be stood up at some restaurant somewhere, stirring some pathetic spoon in his Penne Vodka and wondering what he did wrong.

I was not a fan of this.

Right before I closed the door to my History class, I caught a quick glimpse of Carmen. She had some braids in her hair that looked utterly beautiful. She had a semi sheer stocking on that made her legs look shimmery and there was no way they were up to uniform code. In fact, half the things that Carmen wore had to break Saint Lawrence rules – the jangly jewelry and the scarves. It was as though they let her wear what she wanted because she was Fashion Chair and couldn't be chained to uniforms. What a life...

I decided Mr. Mayer would recover from one no-show date.

I got a "C" on my History test. Not very good. Better than I thought, sadly. Mr. Walsh hated me more than any of my other teachers but that was only because he had the misfortune of being my first class. I knew I had to get in good graces with him. I had to get in good graces with a lot of people lately.

Which reminded me. Abby. What to do about Abby? Maybe wait until the Macs party when most of the girls are drunk and then ask why they don't like her? But then they may not remember the conversation, in which case it'll do no good. Abby, Abby, Abby—

Amanda Betancourt. Twelve o'clock. Now was the time to say something. If I really belonged in a group of girls like MASCARA, I'd have the nerve to walk right up to her and defend my friend. I straightened my spine as I thought about my being tougher and stronger and nervier. I breathed in a long inhale. I thought hard about taking the inevitable punishment of being late to yet another class if I deterred and asked

Amanda Betancourt, who wasn't my biggest fan either, why she didn't like Abby. I had almost, and I mean almost, mustered up the courage to do this when...

I decided to take a different approach. Amanda wasn't my answer. She was off-putting and intimidating (in a bad way, not in an Asher way) and this would go south pretty fast. I had to get in class, scribble about A.D. versus B.C. and think of who my best play was.

I scurried into my desk and unpacked my books neatly.

"Hey, are you like exempt from Senior Slave Day tomorrow or what?" I heard a voice whisper.

I turned toward a frail girl sitting diagonally from me. She had a safety pin in her ear.

"No, why would I be?" I asked.

"You're part of that group right? Mascara or lipstick or whatever the Hell they are," she said.

As if she didn't know.

"Not quite. And it's MASCARA," I answered.

The girl was furiously biting at her nail.

"Right," she said.

I turned back to the front of the room and started etching down names like they were schematics for my new house. Did I talk to Carmen's sister? She had a ton of loose advice to throw around. Maybe I could even talk to Carmen. No. What about Liam's sister Aimee? Talking to alumni probably broke all kinds of MASCARA rules. No, that was an awful idea. It would make them look bad to the alumni.

Could I talk to Asher? Should I talk to Asher?

I continued to doodle while safety pin girl continued to inspect me. I didn't have to see her doing it, I felt her.

I wondered how I was going to get Mr. Mayer to agree to go out with me. It didn't hurt to send a quick message from the bathroom and make sure I asked him out first. Did it?

I raised my hand. "May I have the hall pass?"

Gym class was about forty times harder than it normally was. Mr. Mayer seemed like he was in much brighter spirits and the poor sap had no idea that he was being wooed by fake women. He thought he was popular. Really popular.

Funny what that could do to a person.

I felt bad for him during jumping jacks. I felt bad for him running laps. I felt bad for him picking teams. I felt bad for him playing volleyball. I literally felt bad for him the entire duration of my gym class, which was like 42 minutes – a long time to feel bad for someone.

When I went to the locker room to change, I grabbed my phone from my bag and logged in to see if he had written me back, despite how truly bad I felt.

CityMayer: How's seven tonight?

There it was. I was going to win this task. I had secured a good old non-date date between CityMayer and LuLuForYou. Where should they not go? Should they not have Italian?

I began typing back as fast as my hands could move.

LuLuForYou: Seven is great. Italian?

I felt triumphant. I felt like I was not only going to win this task and get out of any pledge task I wanted but I was on my way to meet Asher and get incredibly amazing clothes to wear tomorrow for Dress Down Day and even though tomorrow was Senior Slave Day, I didn't care. It was a day closer to my first ever Macs party and I couldn't wait to spend some real time around Derek. Somehow.

I walked extra quickly toward the senior hallway, enthusiastic to share the news with Asher that Mr. Mayer picked me and we would not have Italian and not slurp a single spaghetti noodle together like "Lady and the Tramp" and then not end the night with some smooching. My not date was going to be sooo romantic.

I charged through the parking lot like I owned the thing. Who did I think I was? Seriously, I had been in this lot once. I didn't care, I was too excited.

I spotted Asher's white shiny car from the door. I watched on both sides as everyone began to strip their uniform pieces off and start to resemble individuals more, sheep a little less.

I was completely buzzing by the time I saw Asher.

"Guess what?" I said.

"You look awfully chipper," Asher said. She was sorting through clothes in her backseat.

"Mr. Mayer picked me! He's going to go on a date with me tonight," I said. "Well, Lulu not me but you know what I mean."

Asher turned and looked at me. She looked incredibly unimpressed.

She groaned. "Ugh, what scum he is," she said.

I was lost. And a little offended. Was he scum just because he picked me? Well, because he picked Lulu? Lulu was really the winner here.

"He picked all of you," Asher said. "He gave you all time slots that are like an hour and a half apart."

"Wait. He's going out with four women in a single night?"

"That we know of. Maybe there's more we don't even know about. Well, technically he's going out with no women, that we know of, because technically you are all fake. But, in his mind, yes."

"What an ass!" I exclaimed.

"Exactly. A two-timing ass. A four-timing ass," Asher said.

"So what does this mean for the task?" I asked.

"Unfortunately, it means you all win which kind of means you all lose."

"Can I tell him he's an ass?" I asked Asher.

"No, because how would you know," she said and handed me a t-shirt.

I opened the shirt. Cold Pizza.

"What's cold pizza mean?"

"It's my boyfriend's band. Wear that tomorrow. With these."

Asher handed me a pair of gray corduroys with a few small tears by the kneecap. I held them up to my waist. I had no idea if they'd fit me or not. Asher was taller and thinner than I was.

"Okay," I said.

"And this," she said and extended a navy cardigan.

I took the sweater over my arm.

"Got it," I said.

"You need a necklace. Shoot. Let me text Carmen and see what she can bring by my house."

Asher started punching requests into her phone and I stood there like a doll. I pictured her brushing my hair with one of those Victorian hair-brushes with painted roses and thick bristles then laying out all of the frilly doll clothes I would wear.

I was a puppet. A pledge. A pawn. I felt kind of dirty.

The only person I could take this frustration out on was Mr. Mayer.

"Is there anything we can do to him? Maybe later on or even next year? Or online? He can't just four time girls! He's not even cute!"

"Oh, I'm sure we will figure something out. Don't forget, our Contact Chair has thousands, and I mean literally thousands, maybe *tens* of thousands of email addresses. Everywhere we go we make friends with important people and add them to the MASCARA email list. There are very brutal things we can do to Mr. Mayer, just wait."

Carmen ran up to us during our vengeance plot.

"He gave you the seven o'clock?" Carmen asked laughing. "What a pimp Mr. Mayer is!"

"Ew," Asher said.

My sentiments exactly.

Carmen handed a chain link necklace to Asher who then handed it to me.

"Are you dressing Missy today?" she asked Carmen.

"Mmhmm," she said.

Great. If *Carmen* was dressing Missy Warwick then Missy Warwick was not going anywhere soon. I wanted to scream. First I feel bad for Mr. Mayer who is nothing more than a 17-year old player in the body of an old gym teacher and now my plan to eliminate Missy was foiling all around me. She was probably going to look stunning tomorrow after Carmen got through with her. And I still hadn't helped the Abby thing one bit.

"Thanks, for the necklace," I said to Carmen.

Carmen smiled but didn't say anything else.

"Always," said Asher.

"Always," Carmen said back to her.

I couldn't tell how I felt about the "always" thing. In theory, it was kind of dumb. But somehow, I still wanted to say it.

"Okay, get in," Asher said to me.

I rushed around to the passenger side, God willing, where I would stay. No driving for me today.

Asher got in the car. She primped in the mirror before putting the key in the ignition. Why does this girl primp at all? She had absolutely zero need to do anything because she fell out of bed perfect. But despite how pretty all of the girls in MASCARA were, it dawned on me they'd be kind of boring without all the fluff. The blue lashes and the accessories and Cold Pizza bands and chair positions. It was all the extra layers of amazing that made them who they were. Did I have extra layers of amazing?

"Jorie," Asher said, in a way like she had been calling me for minutes.

"Huh?"

"Tomorrow you're going to get another task in your locker. I'm really not supposed to be telling you that. Make sure you wear this outfit well. Do whatever the seniors ask you but don't hesitate to stick up for yourself if it's demoralizing in any way. And whatever you do, don't stay home. Freshman that stay home get it ten times worse."

I paid attention to her every word.

"Even if they are truly sick?"

"Don't even think about it," Asher said.

"Oh I'm not, not for m—"

Asher's phone started ringing. Surprise, surprise. She put the phone on speaker so she could drive.

The next thing I heard come over the car was:

"Hey gypsy its Mara. I think we have grounds to blackball one of the girls. I'm not on speaker right?"

Asher pushed a button.

"Yes, hold on," she said.

Suddenly I felt sick to my stomach. Who was getting blackballed? I went through my mental Rolodex of the rules I could remember. Did I break one? I shifted uncomfortably in my seat.

Asher listened in the phone, now off speakerphone.

"Are you sure about this?" she asked.

A pause.

"Like absolutely no doubt about it positive?"

Another pause.

"I'll look into it. Call you later. Always."

Asher drove silent for a second.

"MASCARA needs to have an emergency meeting tonight. We may have an issue. Keep your phone on."

"Is everything alright?"

"I don't know," was all she said. The rest of the way home we drove in silence.

"Remember, keep your phone on," Asher said as I was getting out of the car with all of her clothes in my hand.

"Thanks for the ride," I said and slammed the door.

I had half a mind to go meet Mr. Mayer at the Italian restaurant and punch him in the face for this day. At least Lulu would get her last laugh.

CHAPTER 15

I got the call that changed everything around 9 p.m. I had tried on the cold pizza shirt with non-matching cardigan and corduroy pants like five times already. I had put on my blue mascara and wiped it off with the wipey things that I never used before this part of my life. I paced my room and I sat cross-legged on my floor and tried to find videos of Cold Pizza online. I fiddled with my hair in the mirror. I text Abby and asked her if she wasn't feeling well since she didn't appear to have to come to school today. I spent a solid half hour with my dad at dinner (warm pizza) because my mom took Matt to see a movie that he wanted to see.

My heart was beating out of my chest at like a million miles a minute. Then the unthinkable happened.

My phone chimed. It was Asher.

"Hello?"

"Marjorie?"

"Asher. Hi."

"We have a problem."

"Is it Mr. Mayer? Are we caught? He tracked our IP addresses," I said quickly into the phone.

As bad as it thought it would be if that were true, it didn't compare to what actually came out of Asher's mouth.

"It's your friend Abby. Well, I guess former friend Abby. She has come to MASCARA with some alarming claims about you."

I dropped my phone. As in, to the ground. I actually and literally dropped my phone out of shock.

I slowly bent down and picked it up.

"Hello? Jorie?"

"I'm here," I said, in a complete stupor.

"At first we thought she was just desperate to get a bid. I mean she has been asking us every day since Recruitment Day. Saying that you didn't really want to be in MASCARA anyway. But, then she told Amanda and Mara that you were talking about them behind their backs. That you text her constantly about us and just wanted to get in to change everything. Things like that."

Was I hallucinating? How could this be happening? The very same girl that I had been friends with for ten years? That I Trick-or-Treated with in joint costumes? That I've stuck up for on countless occasions? That I've shared all of my secrets with?

"Are you sure about this?" I asked her. My voice was shaking.

"I'm sure. It's not true right?" Asher asked.

My brain was in a blender.

"Not true? Asher, she has been telling me that she was getting bullied by you guys for weeks! That the girls were making her cry and she wanted to *transfer schools* because of it."

"You never mentioned any of that before," Asher said.

"This is crazy. Abby told me one of you must have had a thing for her boyfriend Jake. That she got made fun of..."

"She told us that you were the kind of girl to steal someone's boyfriend. That you flirted with Jake right in front of her. Offered him liquor or something. That you said Amanda was a bitch. I even think she showed Amanda some text, which doesn't look good Jor."

She called me Jor. Not Marjorie.

"Asher, I swear to you, all of this is a lie. I may have tried to make Abby feel better when she said that she was bullied to tears but I never once talked bad about MASCARA or did any of the things she said I did."

"But if your best friend was being bullied to tears, wouldn't you ask us why?"

"I was trying to find the right time. Without getting myself kicked out of the pledge program."

"Listen Jor, I want to believe you. I do believe you. It's her word against yours and we don't know her. But I only have one vote. For now, just continue pledging as usual and at the monthly meeting Sunday, we'll have to vote on the blackball. Try to find proof that Abby is lying, okay?"

My eyes welled with tears. I'd been stabbed in the back by my own best friend just so she could *steal* my other friends. Was there any feeling in the world worse than that? What kind of demon person would do that? She played both sides of the fence or the coin or whatever it is that someone does when they spread lies to two sides.

Evil.

I felt bad for Mr. Mayer and he turned out to be a womanizing juggler. I felt bad for Abby and she had been playing me the entire time to try and get her bid for MASCARA. She had faked tears in front of my own mother!

I was so angry I ripped down every photo I had with Abby attached to my mirror. All of the color and black and white strips from photo booths going as far back as fifth grade. All crinkled. All lies.

I threw the make-up kit that Abby bought me for my birthday in the garbage.

I was about to text her when I stopped and thought about it for a minute. If I text her now, I blew any chance of figuring out something better. If she knows that I know, game over.

I decided to hang Abby up with Mr. Mayer on the "I'll figure it out later" hook.

Think Marjorie, think.

Tomorrow was Senior Slave Day. I was going to get it bad from Mara, I just knew it. There was no way she would believe me. Thankfully Amanda Betancourt was a junior or I'd have her to deal with too.

Then I remembered that Asher told me a critical piece of advice.

Don't skip school tomorrow or I would get it ten times worse later...

I picked up my phone, which incidentally had no text back from Abby. The last text sent was mine asking if she wasn't feeling well. How thoughtful of me to my sadistic friend.

I typed away:

Well, hope you feel better. You should stay home tomorrow. If you miss Senior Slave Day, you totally get off the hook. Feel better! ☺

Send.

If Abby could lie to me, then I could lie to her.

It was weird to wear Asher's clothes to school. For starters, it was the type of outfit I would never wear. Or at least I wouldn't think to buy its pieces. But I knew from the way that girls looked at me today that they would be trying to find navy cardigans or corduroy pants by the week-end if not sooner. That was at least half the school's response – people wanted to copycat my clothes right off my body. Well, her clothes.

The other half knew that they were Asher's clothes. It was as though she made sure I wore the Cold Pizza t-shirt so that everyone knew which doll was hers on the shelf. I felt kind of violated when I thought of it like that.

"Is that the band, Cold Pizza?"

I'd nod.

"With Frankie Ford? Right on," said Boy I Never Spoke To Before (or After).

I'd nod again and keep walking the catwalk.

"Pledge!" I heard from somewhere close.

It was Mara. She had on a white t-shirt that she chopped up with scissors that said SENIORS across the breast in maroon. Everyone was wearing them today to make some sort of statement.

Her hair was pulled into a messy bun and her prominent features were even more prominent.

"Pledge, carry my books to my classroom, right over there, room 312," she said and pointed sharply.

I hated when she called me Pledge or Pledgling.

"Sure," I said. What else could I say to this?

"Don't roll your eyes at me either, pledge."

"I, I didn't," I stammered.

"Are you answering back?"

How did I get here?

I tilted my head down and walked to room 312 with Mara's entire collection of schoolbooks. She had every subject in that pile for a single class. Not likely.

I placed them down on an empty desk and rushed off before I was late for History.

Abby wasn't at her locker. Which was just as well. She deserved the karma of a double Senior Slave Day.

The more I thought I about it, the angrier I was. Why couldn't she just be supportive from the start?

I realized I was marching my feet just a little as I walked, like a pouty infant. I felt like a pouty infant. In cool clothes.

Right before I made it to my hallway I felt a pull on my bag strap. It was Derek.

"Good luck today kid," he said. He smiled his lethal smile that he knew very well was lethal.

"Thank you!" I called back, still in my pouty infant mode, just less pouty.

The air just hung with torment. It smelled of freshman fear and senior laughter. This was going to be a very, very long day.

"Lunch. Now. Something healthy," Mara said at the start of fourth period.

Somehow Mara was really the only one giving me grief. Surprise.

I'm sure if any of the other members of MASCARA were seniors they'd be putting me through Hell too. But, the other (non MASCARA) members of the senior class really hadn't ordered me around much. I had to hand deliver a note to someone for someone before second period, steal a hall pass pad before Lit class, and guard the bathroom door for the last ten minutes while some girl did who knows what.

This was all after a speech in Homeroom from my teacher on how Senior Slave Day doesn't really exist and no one should do anything that they are told to do by another student.

I waited in the lunch line for Mara and tried to figure out what in this line of slop was healthy. Liam walked up behind me.

"So who's lunch are you getting?" he laughed while he spoke.

"Mara French's," I said. "You?"

"My own," Liam said.

I raised an eyebrow.

"Everyone in this school takes it easy on me because of Aimee. I kind of hate it. I want my own experience."

"Do you want to take Mara French her lunch, because I have no problem with helping you on your journey. Ya know, for the experience," I said jokingly.

"Oh you're quick today Carr," Liam said.

Again, I noticed how incredibly obviously good-looking he was. But still, not my type. Who was I kidding? I had no type. I was just tunnel-visioned on Derek Mackey.

"I'm in a mood," I said.

"Of course you are, it's Senior Slave Day baby!"

I kind of wanted to tell him that it wasn't just that. To confide in him. To talk to someone about what my own best friend had done to me. Pontius Pilate Abby Port threw me to the wolves.

"I've gotta get this to Mara before she implodes," I said instead.

I carried the grimy tray over to where Mara was standing next to Adrianna and placed it on the table in front of them.

"Oh, I'm not actually going to eat that. C'mon pledge do you think I'd eat anything off of a tray?"

I just wasted my own money. I decided maybe I'd sit and eat the disgusting grimy tray food that I paid for.

As I went to sit, Mara stopped me.

"Go sneak into the boys bathroom and see if anyone is talking about me, us."

"How am I supposed to do that?" I asked, half-thinking she was kidding.

"I don't know, figure it out," Mara answered.

Adrianna looked at me somewhat sympathetically. It didn't last long.

"Are you going to the emergency meeting Sunday night?" Mara asked Adrianna.

Zing.

I decided sneaking into the boy's bathroom would be much less humiliating than where this conversation was headed.

"I'll let you know what I hear," I said.

Mara gave me a look. "I know you will."

"I love those pants! Even though I know they're not yours!" Adrianna called as I was walking out, to show she was human.

That was sadly the best she could come up with.

I am crouched on a men's room toilet. Can this day get more disgusting? I spent my entire lunch period crouched on a dirty, smelly men's room toilet just waiting for boys to come in and talk. Because that's what so many boys do when they pee, make small talk about the girls they like. Was Mara crazy? This wasn't social tea hour.

I had to get out of here. I had nothing to report and I had to get out of here. I felt blessed to have pants blocking any part of my actual skin from touching any part of this experience.

I was peering through the door crack, (apparently I was getting good at this angle), when I heard his voice.

No, no, no.

As if this 24 hours could get any more warped than it already was.

Derek was walking into the bathroom. There was simply no way I could take my eyes off the door now.

"So what are you gonna do man?"

"What can I do? I'm asking her to go," Derek said.

"You can't though," the other boy said.

"Why?"

"You know why."

"I'm asking her anyway, I have to."

Derek was now facing a urinal and I had to close my eyes. I had to. This was all wrong. I didn't want to hear him pee before I ever even kissed him. Come to think of it, I really didn't want to hear him pee after I kissed him either. This day really needed to end quicker.

I was now sweating. I had to get out of there and make it to Spanish class in the next three minutes. How was I supposed to walk out? What if a teacher was outside of there?

Derek and his buddy continued to talk but about some sports game and I lost interest. Could they take any longer?

Yes, it was an unbelievable play Derek, now get out.

I couldn't help but wonder, he couldn't ask who to what?

CHAPTER 16

"Take Out Missy Warwick"

Getting out of the boy's bathroom was no easy feat. I almost got myself busted, twice.

"Love your outfit!" some girl said as she walked by.

I was too distracted to respond. Who was Derek asking somewhere? I rushed to Spanish class asking myself the same thing over and over. I was actually now trying to figure out how to ask it in Spanish. Donde? Was that "where?" How do I say "who?"

No wonder I was getting the grades I was getting...

I finally saw Asher just before I crept into class, but only for a brief second. "Did you find any proof about Abby?" she whispered.

"Not yet. I think she ditched school today," I said back.

"Okay, get to class. Nice clothes by the way," she said.

"Ha. Thanks," I said back.

She looked like a stylist spent the morning with her. Her long hair was curled into big, loose curls at the bottom. She wore a black and white polka dotted halter top with black shorts over black leggings and boots.

Who thinks of these things? My shorts were already packed away for the season.

⁂

I sat in Spanish class pretending to conjugate verbs and trying to figure out how to prove my innocence with this Abby thing. If I showed them the exchange of texts, I would also have to show them the text where I called Amanda Betancourt a bitch and that was concrete proof that I talked bad about someone in MASCARA. I couldn't rely on texts. I needed better.

With all the bustle of the day, I forgot that I had pulled another blue envelope from my locker this morning.

Azul?

I slid the envelope from the front pouch of my bag underneath my notebook and onto my desk. Very quietly, I slit the top of the envelope with my fingernail. The last thing I needed now was for one of these cards to get taken away by a teacher.

I maneuvered the card out under a sheet of notebook paper.

Pledges,

As you all know, Mr. Mayer is a four date in one night kind of guy so your last task is basically null and void. From here on out, your tasks will be together not against one another. You will have one this afternoon, but you will have each other to lean on. It's only one hour after school and you're home free to go the party tomorrow night at the Mackey's. P.S. We had an internal issue we are working out through emergency meetings. Please ignore any rumors, we will have a decision Sunday on how to proceed.

Always,
MASCARA

I read it three times back to back. In three days I could be kicked out of this pledge program all because of Abby. All the hard work I had put in, all the risks I had taken. No. I couldn't let that happen. If I couldn't figure out how to get Abby to confess, I had to figure out how to get Missy Warwick to drop. If they have no other "M" name, they have to take me. If they have the option of taking Missy over me, I didn't stand a chance.

Then I remembered I hadn't seen her Carmen-designed outfit yet today. Come to think of it, I hadn't seen her at all today. Who doesn't make sure they are seen every minute of a day when they are in Carmen Banks' clothes? An idiot. An idiot that didn't deserve to be in MASCARA. That's who.

I folded up the card and tucked it away. I decided to pay attention to at least some of this class. I was supposed to keep a "B" average after all.

After three more hours of carry this, fetch that, come here, go there – school was finally letting out for the day. It wasn't really that bad, all things considered. I had to do ten push ups in the hallway which was kind of gross because the floors in the hallway were gross but other than that, I got out alive.

I never once saw Abby or for that matter Missy Warwick. I was dreading seeing how good Missy looked in Carmen's clothes. I did, however, get a kick out of how sullen Mr. Mayer seemed today in gym class. His big shiny smile from yesterday had been robbed by a thief in the night. Or four thieves. Four fake girlfriends all stood him up. He must have wondered how in the world he could have gotten so damn unlucky.

He did give us extra exercises as a punishment for his own moral bad judgment. I snickered to myself through the entire class. Well, most of the class. I spent a few too many minutes wondering if Asher's clothes were safe in the locker room. As though some caper would break into my combination lock (with a crowbar not a combination) and rob Asher's threads. I pictured this in between my extra exercising and laughing at Mr. Mayer.

The parking lot was filled with the same white and maroon SENIORS t-shirt over and over and over. In fact, that was all I could really see, a sea of SENIOR shirts. Finally, I spotted Andy Flynn and Ashley Walker standing on the side of Mara's car. I only prayed we wouldn't get asked to wash it or something equally ridiculous.

"Pledges, get in," Mara said.

Still no sign of Missy Warwick. Odd. I piled into the backseat with Andy and Ashley.

Asher was walking over to meet Mara, she had something in her hands.

"Any of you see Missy today?" I asked once the doors were closed and Mara was out of earshot.

"She was a no show. Can you believe that! She was supposed to wear Carmen's clothes and she no showed!" said Andy.

Ashley piped in, "She text me around lunch time and said that we were dumb for coming. That if we didn't come in today we would have been totally off the hook."

"Off the hook? You get it ten times worse if you cut school on Senior Slave Day," I said.

Wide-eyed, they both stared at me.

"Really?"

"How do you know?"

I couldn't tell them Asher told me. She wasn't supposed to tell me.

"I heard it from a few juniors," I lied.

I wondered why Missy would have thought she would be totally off the hook. Totally off the hook? Weren't those the exact words I said to Abby when I text her about staying home? That she'd be totally off the hook...

Right then, Asher got in the car.

"Each of you take one of these and secure it around your eyes," she said.

I pawed for whatever was in her hand, not sure what she was talking about. They were long blue strips of silk.

I take that back. They were blindfolds.

I shot a look of pure petrification to Andy. Ashley had already covered her eyes with the material and was awkwardly trying to tie a knot in the back of her head.

Andy turned and took the loose ends from Ashley's hands and helped her secure a knot.

Why were we being blindfolded? I somehow doubted we were being brought to some calm, serene spa somewhere and relaxing to the sounds of waterfalls and Amazon rain.

I wrestled with the silk to get it across the front of my face and tightly pulled the ends around the back of my head.

Andy took my two ends the same way she had Ashley's and began to tie a knot evenly in the middle of my head.

There. Now I couldn't see a thing.

"How you girls doing?" Mara asked.

Her voice, from behind a blindfold, was much, much scarier.

"Good," Andy said. I assumed she had tied her own knot.

Damn Girl Scout.

"Where's Missy?" Asher asked.

"Oh you didn't check the app I guess. Missy decided not to show today. Stayed home 'sick' apparently. Where *did* we get this crop of pledges this year? They're awful," Mara said.

"Mara be nice," said Asher.

"No offense!" Mara called to us, as though she hadn't ever offended us until this moment.

"Wow, why would Missy stay home?" Asher asked. "Any of you girls know? You should be leaning on one another by now."

Ashley told them what she had told us minutes ago. That Missy assumed she was "totally off the hook." That phrase was bothering me. It was sitting in this weird part of my stomach and just remaining there, like bad Mexican food.

Somewhere in the same part of my stomach, was the fact that Derek was asking someone to go somewhere and it most certainly wasn't me. Or maybe it was me and that's why "he couldn't" because, I can't? Was that far-fetched? I was beginning to confuse myself.

Mara was driving and I was blindfolded and all I could see was black nothingness and all I can smell was perfume and Candy Cane air freshener and all I can feel was the light air from the vent coming out near my kneecap.

Where were we going?

The car came to an abrupt halt about ten minutes later. Not one person spoke the entire car ride.

"Okay girls, you can lower your blindfolds for a minute," Mara instructed.

We all began to exit the car and loosen the silk around our eyes.

"Don't take them off, just lower them so you can put them back on," Asher said.

Andy, Ashley and myself just stood confused. We were in front of what looked like a burnt down movie theater.

"Welcome to Satan's Palace," Mara said.

"Huh?" I let out.

Mara smiled. "Satan's Palace," she reiterated.

"What's Satan Palace?" Ashley asked.

Asher looked less impressed. "It's just a local horror story. This place was a movie theater forty years ago and there was a major fire that tore through it."

"What does that have to do with Satan?" Andy asked.

I was thinking the same question.

I was waiting for Mara to grow horns or take out her tail. Prod us with a pitchfork maybe.

"Supposedly, people have practiced black magic in here ever since," Asher added. "Mara, will you take them in, I don't want to rip these leggings."

"Gladly," Mara said.

She stood on some sort of cinder block and hoisted a leg up to a window, then shimmied herself over. There were boards on all of the other windows and the door. There were signs from the city, generic KEEP OUT signs; basically every which way you can tell someone not to go in somewhere, it was posted.

"I'll see you girls in an hour," Asher said. "Oh and Jorie, don't get my pants dirty!"

An hour?!

I pulled myself into the small window space that Mara had so easily fit through.

Andy and Ashley were right behind me.

It was pretty dark inside anyway, though there were several beams of light playing peek-a-boo. When the light shone right, I could see all kinds of graffiti and triple 6's along the walls. There were charred seats in rows and tons of cigarette butts and stubbed-out joints on the ground. The place was filthy and crawling with who knows what.

An eerie feeling hung in the air, both for the fire and for all of the worshipping that has gone on since. It was the type of place you see in horror movies where someone has an animal on a spit over a fire and a "6" tattooed under their eye or something. I got a chill down the middle of my spine.

"Ladies, you are to spend an hour in here, on the clock, blindfolded. This will force you to talk to each other and lean on each other and hopefully you will bond. Don't get bit by anything creepy and don't bother screaming – no one can hear you," Mara said. "Blindfolds up! See you all in an hour!"

What was I doing here? What was I doing here? What was I doing here?

I wanted to sit down before I hyperventilated but what would I sit on? A fried half-chair? Plus, Asher told me not to get her pants dirty.

"This sucks," I said out loud.

Ashley and Andy laughed. I couldn't tell exactly where they were but they were somewhere in front of me, probably about five feet away.

"Did you hear that?" Ashley asked.

"No," I said.

"I did," said Andy.

"Hear what?" I asked.

"It sounded like a hissing," Ashley said.

"Wonderful," I said.

This was going to be the longest sixty minutes of my life.

I learned about something called "trauma bonding" in Psychology class this week. It's when you go through traumatic experiences with other individuals and it can bond you for life. Like your platoon or whatever.

I started picturing Andy and Ashley and myself in fatigues, rolling around on the ground with war paint on our faces and hiding from the enemy. Andy would move out and fire off a few shots, then duck back for cover with us. Ashley would likely get shot and I would just lay there shocked and trying to say the right things to her. "Stay with us!" I'd say. She'd then tell me it was "so cold."

I couldn't afford to daydream like that while I was standing up and blindfolded. The likelihood was high that I would drift off and fall on my face. In this disgusting Satanic mess of a place.

"Anyone want to play a game?" I asked.

By the time Mara came back in to let us know our time in hell was up, we were all hysterical laughing and genuinely having the time of our lives. I don't think Mara was pleased about this.

"Looks like you guys are having fun," she said. "You can lower your blindfolds."

I was still short of breath from laughing so hard. I actually and truly liked Ashley *and* Andy. Who knew?

We were so jumpy from all of the bugs that we were convinced were landing on us or sucking our blood and burrowing through our ear ways that we made a game of it. A game guessing the amounts of legs and antennae on the mystery insects sucking our blood or laying nests in our hair.

I honestly didn't want to leave them.

"Get in the car," Mara said.

We all climbed out through the small open window that we came in through and walked to Mara's car. Asher was in shotgun with a clipboard.

"Nice job girls," she said. "Now, you will have to fill Missy in on your next task but don't tell her about Satan's Palace, she'll have to do it alone."

"Alone?" I asked.

"Her own fault. Not our problem. She decided to ditch school," Asher said.

Mara made a face that clearly said, "*too bad*."

Asher handed me a clipboard.

"Tomorrow, you girls need to put the school up for sale. I don't care how you do it. I don't care where you do it. Advertise online, put signs on the property, get a realtor for all I care. Just make sure the Dean is getting calls asking for the sale price of the school by Monday."

And there went the good mood that Andy, Ashley and myself had found. Right out the window.

CHAPTER 17

By the time I got home, I was exhausted and smelled like burnt upholstery. I didn't look so hot either.

Now I had to figure out how to put the school up for sale, which was both hilarious and ludicrous at the same time.

"Mom, I'm going to sleep at Asher's tomorrow night. We have a birthday party to go to. At our friend Adrianna's house," I said.

"You most certainly won't be," my mom said, without stopping to look at me. She stood cutting celery into small even pieces.

"What do you mean?"

"What do you mean what do I mean? Are you telling me what your plans are or asking for permission? You were late to work last week Marjorie," my mom started.

"By like five minutes. You can't be serious," I said defensively.

"As a heart attack. You're welcome to go to your friend's birthday party and your father or I will pick you up at ten," my mom said.

"Ten!"

"Fine. Ten-thirty. What does cold pizza mean anyway?"

I ignored her.

This was mortifying. If I wanted to go to the first ever Macs party and likely the only one I would ever be invited to in my entire life once I got blackballed on Sunday, I had to leave with my mommy or daddy at 10:30!

I stormed out of the kitchen. My mother was being completely unreasonable. I had been late to a store that sold water by five lousy minutes. It wasn't like there was a drought in Willow Grove and the whole town was lining up outside the store with their tongues out just waiting for us to quench their thirst.

I marched up the steps and into my room and locked my door. I had homework to do. Real homework. For school, so I didn't fail these classes. And I had to start researching land prices and places to advertise said school. I figured we had to do any advertising online from the school computers so none of us get tracked to our houses.

I put down my books and bag and clipboard and sat on my bed. I was sad to take Asher's clothes off but I really wanted to be comfortable. I hung the cardigan on my door and peeled off the rest to go into laundry. I wanted my own pair of corduroys. Maybe I'd use my gift card for *Sigh* and buy some. If I had anyone to go to the mall with...

As it turns out, it's tough to sell a school. To really sell one, not fake sell one.

There was a big part of me that wanted to post a bunch of advertisements for the school and say to call the gym teacher. It served Mr. Mayer right for trying to four time a bunch of very nice non-existent women.

I invested most of my night in learning municipal real estate instead of Geometry or History. I knew my report was falling behind but if I was going to be blackballed in under three days, I would have all the time in the world to concentrate on my academics for the rest of high school.

I couldn't sleep at all that night. I was thinking about Abby, then Derek in the bathroom (in a non gross way), then Mr. Mayer (also in a non gross way), then Missy, then today at Satan's Palace, then cold pizza (the food not the band).

I was upset about so many things I didn't even know where to begin. How was I going to pull off leaving this party tomorrow night at 10:30 without being completely and utterly humiliated?

I managed to finally get a few broken up hours of sleep, between flipping my pillow two hundred times to find the cool side, throwing off the blankets, pulling back on the blankets and finally, wishing my alarm clock would explode.

Somewhere during that time I actually had a dream I could remember. A dream that made so little sense, I had to wonder if I touched some sort of crazy potion at Satan's Palace.

I was a sheep herder. I was actually bringing a herd of sheep to this abandoned farm that looked like it had had a fire in it. I stopped midway through the grass and let three cats walk by before continuing with my sheep. When I finally got them to the barn, I started brushing their backs with a mascara brush. I was painting them all blue. One of the cats leapt up into the barn window and started hissing at me. It had yellow eyes, mean yellow eyes, and fur that was sticking up on end like it had been electrocuted.

Then I woke up.

"Why would you tell me that I'd be off the hook if I skipped school on Senior Slave Day?" Abby was practically hysterical at my locker on Friday morning. The hissing cat.

As if this was all my fault.

"What are you talking about?" I asked point blank.

"I'm talking about the fact that you lied to me," Abby said, loudly.

"I lied to you? Really, Abby?"

"What's that supposed to mean?"

I kept loading books into my locker so I wouldn't have to look her in the eyes.

"How did I lie to you?" I asked, focused on the inside of my locker.

People were beginning to stare.

"You told me that if I missed Senior Slave Day I would be totally off the hook and I believed you. I even told other people who were afraid to come to school."

"Like Missy Warwick?"

Damn. I didn't want to say it but it just sort of happened.

Abby put on a confused face. I was tired of her delusional victim sob story. "Let me repeat myself, you look confused. You mean like Missy Warwick? These 'people' you also told because they were afraid to come to school?"

Now I looked her dead in the eyes.

Abby darted her eyes to the ground. "So. She's in my class."

"Or you are purposely trying to help her so she gets in and I don't?"

I slammed my locker.

"You know me better than that Jor. I would never do something like that," she lied.

"Who are you Abby? I know everything. I know how you've been begging for a bid and making up lies about me behind my back to MASCARA to make it seem like I badmouthed them. How could you?"

"I, I didn't—"

"And this whole time you are crying to me that you're being bullied? That they make fun of you and make you cry? You should be ashamed of yourself."

"I just, you didn't even care—"

"Save it. If you'll excuse me, I have a school to sell."

Underneath my books, I had a stack of those red and white plastic FOR SALE signs you buy for a car or a motorcycle.

I had taken them this morning from the garage just in case. I barely spoke to my mother through breakfast. I had gulped down my orange juice and grabbed a muffin to go. If she couldn't see how she was single-handedly ruining my life tonight, then I had nothing to say to her.

I thought she may have budged before I got on the bus but she never did. So I stole her FOR SALE signs. My entire reputation in exchange for her plastic dollar store signs? Seems like she made out in this trade.

I was actually excited to do this task as a pledge class. Together, instead of competing like we had all been doing since day one. Although, if we did compete, I would totally kick everyone's ass because I knew so much about real estate now.

I was about to walk into class when I heard Ashley calling my name.

"Hey Jorie, congrats!"

I didn't know what she was talking about. The yelling match with Abby? Was that rumor already around Saint Lawrence? Stealing my mom's signs successfully?

"Thanks," I said and walked into History. I was too tired to ask her what she was talking about.

Mr. Walsh gave me another frowny face. I wasn't even late today but I'm sure my sheep herding dreams and interrupted sleep had me looking like I was homeless or something.

"Ms. Carr, are you with us?"

Such a dumb question. I was about to snap back the obvious when I saw Asher in the hallway waving me to come out of class.

"Actually Mr. Walsh, I'm not feeling so hot. May I go to the restroom?"

"Perhaps you should go to the nurse if you're not feeling well, no?"

"I don't think it's that serous. Thanks."

I got up and retrieved the hall pass. I considered bringing the FOR SALE signs but there was just no good way to get out of the classroom smuggling signs into a bathroom and not look suspicious.

I walked down the hall toward the bathroom a little so that no one in the class could see me right outside with Asher.

"Did you hear?"

"Umm, I assume I didn't. Hear what?"

"Missy Warwick dropped!"

The words took a few seconds to sink in.

"Wait what? Why?"

"Why? Jorie, who cares why! Do you know what this means? It means you're in. Like no more tasks or anything. You don't even have to sell the school, Andy and Ashley have to do it."

I knew I was supposed to be beyond excited but all I could feel was guilt. "Did she drop because of Senior Slave Day?" I asked.

"Marjorie, are you okay? You're not listening. Who cares? The point is, she dropped. This is like the earliest we have ever gotten a pledge to cross over. I mean, technically, you're still a 'MASCARA in waiting' but—"

"What about the Abby stuff? How do I prove that that was all—"

"Already done. Rachel and Amanda overheard you two this morning by your locker. I guess it was obvious to them who was lying. They are *not* happy with your friend Abby."

"She's not my friend," I said.

"Okay well, give me a hug!"

I hugged Asher and legitimately, I was really, really excited. But I also felt wretched about so many things.

"Don't forget to stop by your locker," Asher said.

"Okay, I will."

"Always," she said.

Wow, this was really happening.

"Always," I said back. Which felt really, *really* good. And knowing that the few people eavesdropping in the hallway just overheard me say it, felt really good too.

On my locker was a single blue rose. It was positively gorgeous. I wasn't even sure how flowers got dyed colors like that but I loved it.

I began to gently pull it off my locker when I stopped. Why not leave it on for the rest of the day? Wasn't this my badge of honor? No use rushing to take it off. Stop and smell the roses, right?

Abby and Jake were standing about twenty feet away and I knew they were talking about me. All the more reason to leave the rose up.

I turned and saw Ashley and Andy walking together and shoved my pile of signage into their hands.

"Take these in case you need them."

"Thanks Jor. Congrats," Andy said.

"Do you guys know why Missy dropped? Was it because of Senior Slave Day?" I asked them.

"She said she wanted to do her own thing. But I'm sure she was a little spooked by SSD. Who wouldn't be if they heard they were going to get it ten times worse?"

I thought about Abby and the grave she had dug herself. Not only did she lie to all of MASCARA, but she also was owed a tenfold Senior Slave Day. She really should transfer to Willow Grove.

"Is that rose on your locker from them?" Ashley asked.

"I assume so," I said. I was smiling from ear to ear like a buffoon.

"See ya at the party tonight. And let us know if you know anyone that wants to buy a school!" Andy said as they started off.

I really liked them both. It was a shame they couldn't both get in.

"Hey what time are you guys staying until?" I asked.

"Whenever! I'm sleeping at Andy's and Andy is supposedly sleeping at my house," Ashley turned and said.

"Hmm. Maybe if I buy the school, I can live here and not with my parents. I have to be home early. Work tomorrow."

"Yes! Work! So you *can* buy the school! At least make an offer," Andy said.

CHAPTER 18

"A Series of Almosts"

After school, I couldn't help but call the main line and pretend I was a buyer for the school. I blocked my phone number and disguised my voice.

I said I wanted to purchase the school for 1.9 million dollars. I heard, "Why am I getting all these calls today" before I actually got put on hold. Then I listened to the hold music and thought about what I was going to say. I almost waited, but I chickened out.

I figured I did my due diligence to help Andy and Ashley look like they got buyers.

I almost forgot the blue rose on my locker but I remembered at the last minute. Everyone stared at it on the bus.

I almost convinced my mom to let me "stay at Asher's" but my dad got involved and then that was out the window. He started on the responsibility speech and how if they condoned me being late last week by letting me sleep out, how on Earth would I ever learn. And if I was five minutes late last week then surely I would be ten minutes late this week and then someday, fifteen!

I almost didn't go to the party. I came close to backing out three different times.

The first time was after my parents gave me the speech about responsibility. The second, was when I couldn't find absolutely anything to wear. As in, nothing. I pulled out every single thing in my closet and tried on at least half of them. Why didn't I go to *Sigh* before this party? Oh. Right, because my only friend stabbed me in the back and I had no one to go the mall with.

After I finally found something to wear, I couldn't get my hair right for over 45 minutes. I actually washed it, then blow dried it and then washed it all over again.

Between washes, I almost didn't go again.

But who was I kidding? I had to go. I had no choice but to go. And I had to leave at 10:30. And that was final.

I was almost going to go early so I could give myself some extra time with Derek but then it dawned on me that that would also mean more time with Adrianna and I wasn't completely ready for that. Plus, how would I get there early? I couldn't get dropped off *and* picked up by my parents – one was bad enough.

So I finally decided on a blue top, fitting for the occasion of me becoming a MASCARA. It had buttons on the sleeves, which I liked a lot. It was only a few months old and probably the cutest top I owned. I also wore the belt that Carmen picked out on a tight pair of jeans and boots I wasn't entirely convinced of. They were brown leather with this stitch-like design that I couldn't tell if I liked or not.

I stood in the mirror, silently criticizing. I felt like I was standing on the pages of one of those tabloid magazines where they write things about your outfit underneath like, "Those boots weren't made for walkin'!"

I put two coats of my cobalt mascara on, psychologically I think I finally felt confident enough to wear it now that I knew I was getting in.

I put a few loose curls in my hair, which I never do. It needed something and secretly, I think I was trying to figure out how Asher got those soda can size curls to stay in tact all day long. My curls? Well, they didn't look a thing like Asher's. They looked more like half cooked macaroni.

I still had Asher's cardigan so I threw it over my top, and brought her other now clean clothes out to her car at eight o'clock.

"You ready to take on your first Macs party as an actual member of MASCARA?" she asked as she pulled up.

Absolutely not.

"Absolutely," I said instead.

I got in shotgun of her car and primped in the teeny tiny mirror as soon as I slid in my seat.

"Hey what chair position am I going to hold?" I asked her.

"I think I'm going to make Amanda Betancourt the new Social Chair. Which means you have to take over Contacts. Which is basically just like being in PR. You just have to always meet people and talk to people and make sure you know who's who and keep in touch with them. Get business cards from adults. Send out emails. It's one of the easiest chairs."

I almost asked her who would be Music Chair but I realized we didn't even know who was getting in yet.

Just the idea of Mara gone next year made me feel a little giddy inside.

"You have to come to our meeting on Sunday night and take the minutes. What time are you done working?"

I didn't know what "take the minutes" meant.

"Usually about five or so," I said while I put on yet another lipstick color.

"Perfect. Come to Lila's Nails on Broad Street when you're done. Will your parents drop you off or do you want me to come and get you? Nevermind, I'll come and get you. Bring a notebook."

I almost asked why but then I figured minutes were notes and probably that's what she meant all along and I had absolutely no problem with taking notes at a meeting. This would help me figure out what the heck I needed to shop for.

"Okay sure," I said, while I traced Tangerine Sorbet around the line of my lips in Asher's Mini mirror.

"You're getting awfully dolled up. Is it because you crossed over?"

"Crossed over?"

"Got in. To MASCARA," Asher said, like I was deaf and dumb.

The truth was, I couldn't be happier that I got in to MASCARA. But I was so damn nervous about this party and about seeing Derek and I couldn't process the happy right now. All I could process was my pulse racing and willing my reflection to show someone else. Someone like Lulu. Lulu always got the guy. Well, almost.

I almost declined a beer when I walked in to the Mackey basement, which was the biggest basement I had ever seen in my life. It was like ten mancaves were merged to form one giant playroom and then had a baby with another room and now it was a mutantly large room filled with things to do. There were antique jukeboxes (that worked!) and a movie size screen running a movie and a gym (not like a lone treadmill, a gym) and massage chairs. There was also a long wooden bar that had tons of plastic cups and nut shells and ping pong balls on it. There were at least six couches and every one of them was filled with seniors from my school. I recognized a handful of people who weren't seniors. That was it, a handful.

"There's nothing to be nervous about. You're a MASCARA now," Asher whispered in my ear when we walked in.

Upon her ego boost, I took the beer though I really don't love the taste of beer and shoved a foamy mouthful in my face, careful not to completely take off Tangerine Sorbet.

"Hey, let me get a grit," I heard from across the room. I immediately placed the voice to Derek's.

He. Looked. Incredible.

Wow. I wasn't entirely sure of what a "grit" was but I would give him a hundred if I possessed them.

I started slowly making my way toward his side of the room. I saw a boy hand Derek a cigarette and Derek put it in the right corner of his mouth and light it. Never once did I find smoking the least bit sexy until I saw him do it. This boy could be the poster child for cavities and make them look good.

After almost walking over to him I decided to wait. I took another few sips of beer and watched as Sue and Amanda walked in with Ashley and Andy. They looked even more nervous than me!

"Jorie!"

Ashley said this fairly loud and I saw Derek look up when my name was shouted. It made me feel a sensation of warm through my whole body. I almost acknowledged him but decided to pretend I didn't actually see him yet.

I met Ashley and Andy at the bottom of the stairs. Amanda smiled a smile at me but didn't say anything.

Sue said, "Congratulations."

"Thank you," I said back and took a few more sips of my beer.

I had only two hours at this party and I needed to get Derek alone somehow.

I chit-chatted with Andy and Ashley about how the school for sale thing went and even told them about my almost purchase. The whole time I was looking at Derek out of the corner of my eye but pretending I didn't see him, which is actually really hard to do.

He was playing a game of darts with Adrianna and two other boys I didn't recognize.

Where were their parents? Why didn't anyone have crazy parents but me?

Mara was on the couch obnoxiously making out with Rob like there was no one else in the basement. Even Rachel – manicured, pedicured, pedigreed, groomed Rachel – was tipsy. I watched her while she spilled a little beer on her shirt and then looked around to see if anyone saw her.

I kept nodding and saying things like "that's crazy" to Ashley and Andy while they told me the entire saga of listing the school for sale.

"We came up with 1.8 million at first but then decided we liked 1.9 million better," Ashley said.

"That's crazy."

It wasn't crazy. That's just a thing people say when they aren't listening to you but want you to think that they are and they find what you are saying to be fascinating.

I almost felt drunk. Off half of a beer.

"Jorie! Congrats!" Carmen came over to us carrying a bunch of small glasses spilling with clear liquor. "Here have a shot!"

I almost said no.

Ashley took one glass from Carmen, guzzled it and then quickly drank another one right behind it.

Andy passed.

"I'll have a tiny one, to celebrate."

"It's Tequilla," Carmen said. She dragged out the word like it was pronounced, "ta-keeeeee-la."

I had no idea whether or not I liked Tequilla but I did know that I did not like vomiting and this seemed like an obvious equation.

I almost shot my glass back but instead I sipped it, which honestly wasn't *that* bad. Burned, but wasn't that bad.

Ashley was already getting animated and kind of chatty. I couldn't do chatty right now.

"See you guys in a bit, I'm going to walk around," I said.

Andy looked like I had just stuck her with babysitting a toddler.

I almost cared.

I inched my way ever so slightly toward Derek and the dartboard but I didn't want to talk to him in front of his sister. So I kind of just awkwardly stood in the middle of the room. I took my phone out so I could do that thing you do when you want to look less lonely so you look deeply immersed in your phone.

Who me? No I'm not standing here alone? I'm dealing with something important on my phone.

As I scrolled around on my phone, I noticed my vision was just a little bit off. And by a little bit I mean a lot bit.

Since my parents were going to inevitably have to somehow pick me up from here (sidenote: I still haven't even given them the address) then I would have to stay sober. No more beer for me and certainly no Tequila. And gum, I needed gum.

Derek looked directly at me. We met eyes. We held eye contact for like minutes. Okay, probably ten seconds but ten seconds is a really long time to hold eye contact.

He smiled and jerked his head to the side as if to say, "Come here."

I shook my head. A "no" shake.

He raised an eyebrow. He jerked his head the other direction toward the staircase as if to say, "Come upstairs?"

I nodded. A "yes" nod.

A little while later, I was in Derek Mackey's bedroom. Derek Mackey's totally-what-you-would-picture bedroom lined with trophies of all sizes and kept perfectly in order.

"Congratulations kid, I hear you're a MASCARA," he said.

"In waiting or whatever but yea, thanks," I said.

"So you going to be too cool for me now or what?" he asked.

"Ha! Me? No, of course not."

Derek sat on the bed next to me. I could literally hear my heart thudding.

Say something, say something.

I almost said something. Instead we had a long silent pause. One that meant we should do something now. I felt a flip flop in my stomach. He put his hand on my knee and a tickle shot through my body beginning at my shoulder blades and landing near my thighs. I looked at his lips and traced them silently in my head.

"So you have no rules left to follow then right?" he asked. He moved his hand up about four inches to the bottom of my thigh. I wanted to pause this moment of my life and live it again and again whenever I wanted. The anticipation was delicious.

"No rules," I said. I met his eyes and then started to gently close my own.

I felt him move his upper body closer to me. I nearly felt him breathing. I inhaled his department store counter scent and raised my right hand to touch him. Our lips finally made feather-light contact when—

"Hey Derek is Marjorie in there? Her Dad's here."

I almost kissed Derek Mackey.

CHAPTER 19

"Love Trumps Crush"

I spent the weekend sulking at the water store. I officially hated my parents forever and refused to speak to either one of them. Not only was my dad early picking me up on Friday night, but he did it on purpose. To "show me the value of minutes."

In those minutes, I could have kissed Derek Mackey. Instead, I did the walk of shame out of his house while people whispered to each other that I was getting picked up by my parents.

Asher tried to cheer me up by saying, "The first to leave the party is always the coolest."

On Saturday night there was a Love Trumps Crush show at a local cafe. All of MASCARA was going and I didn't go. I didn't go because I didn't want to explain that I had work on Sunday and my mom was outside.

Apparently, Ashley was spotted at the show making out with some boy with spikey hair and studded jewelry. Just like that, she was black-balled, I think publicly, but I never really asked. I felt bad for her so I didn't want to know.

So, officially, the new members of MASCARA were myself and Andy Flynn. We're the earliest class to ever cross over. Whatever that means. I put my blue dyed rose in a vase on my shelf and I hung every blue card on my mirror where my pictures of Abby and I used to be.

I called Andy to congratulate her over the weekend and see if she wanted to "take the minutes" with me at the MASCARA meeting. She couldn't be more excited and yet I knew she didn't know what take the minutes meant either.

I rode my bike over to meet Andy for a quick slice of pizza before we walked together to Lila's Nails (I bike walked, she walk walked). It was nice to have a friend to eat with and it was nice to not make Asher pick me up.

Andy and I basically watched seven pedicures and seven manicures take place and scribbled down the line up for Fashion Week Milan and tested a few shaving cream samples that Rachel brought. Sue was also putting together a philanthropy event to raise money for recent fire victims so we spent an hour on that, at least.

Andy was named Music Chair (in waiting), which apparently was a fit for her. She even played the drums. Amanda was thrilled to move up to Social Chair next fall so that I could take Contact Chair. I secretly believe this made her like me a thousand times more – the fact that I had no real talent and could only take Contact Chair. It put her one step closer to following in Asher's shoes.

The meeting was a lot of fun. Even Mara was nice to us, apparently her pledging persona was all for show.

It was the kind of night where you begin waiting for the other to shoe to drop because you're used to things being so screwed up and now they're dreamlike and so you know the boogey man is hiding somewhere waiting to poke a pin in it all and deflate your happy place...

Three days later, pictures of MASCARA wound up blasted on social media, under an anonymous account. One was of Mara and Asher, one was of Rachel, Amanda and Carmen and the other was a group shot of everyone.

This may have been no big deal except for the fact that the pictures that were online were *only* stored on the MASCARA app.

"The app was hacked!" Asher yelled through my phone that morning.

Asher went right to her father to see if the app had been compromised or could be compromised but the answer was obvious. There was just no way those specific photos could have gotten released otherwise. Mr. Sutherland would have to tinker with the app for the next few weeks, at least, to secure it better – so it was now down.

Regardless, secrets were stolen and no amount of tinkering was going to fix that. We weren't even sure what the hackers had seen or read. Hell, I hadn't even been on the app yet. I didn't even have a login until next year.

We were going to have to have an emergency meeting, which sounded like they happened quite often.

I was busy staring off into nothing during lunch and stirring a chocolate milk to death when Liam walked up.

"Haven't seen you in days. Congrats by the way. Aimee told me on Friday," he said. He sat.

"Thanks! I'd love to meet your sister someday," I said.

I really wanted to tell him that our app got hacked into but I couldn't. If he told Aimee it would be catastrophic. Not to mention my fault.

I don't know why I always wanted to tell him things. I guess he seemed trustworthy.

"Are you ready for the dance? You got a costume? I should warn you, mine's funny," he said.

"I haven't even thought about the dance," I said, not thinking.

"You haven't? Really?" Liam asked. It was obvious I had hurt his feelings.

"I didn't mean it like that. Just with everything going on, I haven't had time to think of what to wear."

"Well you better start because my costume is hilarious. You know there's a costume contest right?"

"Nope. I know nothing about this dance. Tell me."

"There's a Fall King and Queen announced, seniors only, and then there's three categories of costume contests: most original, scariest and best overall."

I didn't know there was a Fall King and Queen but I had to admit it was kind of funny given all the royal daydreaming I had had during pledging.

"Who will be King and Queen? Asher and Rob?"

"Well, doesn't Rob go out with Mara?"

"Yes," I said finally sipping my over-stirred chocolate milk.

My eyes widened.

Mara was going to hate Asher if Asher won with her boyfriend.

"Who decides?" I asked. I was beginning to love how Liam knew everything.

"Haven't you seen the voting boxes all over school? They look like coffins?"

I almost snorted my milk. "Ha, no."

"I think voting closes today so you'd better get moving."

He smiled. He had really lovely lines when he smiled. My brain immediately jumped to my miskiss with Derek. My moment forever gone. My almost.

"I'll see ya later hon," he said.

Hon. Hon, like honey. Hmm.

I grabbed my phone to read it before lunch was over. I knew I had heard it dinging.

I had a text from Abby:

There's no reason that there can be only one MASCARA sorority in school. You think it's so hard? We can listen to Love Trumps Crush and The Teachers too. Wear our colored make-up. Missy, Anders, Ashley, Sara and myself will be handing out bids next week: purple mascaras. Just a heads up.

I literally couldn't believe my eyes. I blinked somewhere close to ten times just waiting for the message to disintegrate. I had to talk to Asher right away. The comments about Love Trumps Crush and The Teachers? Abby would never know those bands. Was this proof that they hacked into the app?

I could feel my adrenaline rising. They couldn't just "start" their own sorority? That was preposterous.

I packed up and made my way to the door. I saw one of those coffin voter boxes Liam was talking about just before leaving the lunchroom. I grabbed a handful of tiny papers next to it and scribbled Asher on all of them and then dropped them into the box slot.

"There's just no proof Jor. I mean we saw Ashley at Love Trumps Crush over the weekend. So she knows about *them* at least," Asher said.

We were standing in the hallway after I showed her Abby's text.

"But what about them starting their own sorority? I mean, they have cause to hack into the app right there."

"A hundred girls in this school have cause to hack into the MASCARA app. Cause doesn't mean anything."

"Well, them starting another MASCARA sorority is, is—"

"It's crazy Jorie but it's totally possible. Think about it, we did it. I mean, not us but the alumni who started this. Someone has to start it."

"But to use the same name? The same guidelines?" I asked-yelled.

"It's not like we have a patent on the word 'mascara.' It is what it is. Imitation is the sincerest form of flattery."

I couldn't believe she was handling this so well. Was it because she was graduating? She wouldn't have to deal with it once she was gone but I would.

"I have to get to class," I said.

"See if you can figure out who they are going after for their 'C' and 'R' names," Asher said.

"How?"

"I don't know how. It's your grade, you have to overhear something."

My hatred for Abby was growing by the minute. And now, it was also growing for Missy and Anders and Ashley. What a bunch of traitors. Sore losers. They couldn't have the real thing so they just make their own secondhand sorority?

No sooner did I think about them, did I see Missy and Ashley walking together. Come to think of it, their eyelashes were a lilac-y purple. How could I not have noticed that on Anders in homeroom?

They walked by me as though I was invisible. Ashley, who I had just bonded with a week ago over bugs and Satan. This was truly insane. What kind of platoon member just abandons his guys and joins up with the enemy?

I guess she didn't abandon us, we abandoned her by blackballing her, but she shouldn't have broken the rules and made out with some guy.

I thought about it. I was no better. Even if I hadn't crossed over, I would have made out with Derek at the party if my dad hadn't shown up to pick me up. I would have broken the rules, I would have been blackballed. I would probably be begging Abby to take me into MASCARA II.

What am I saying? No I wouldn't have.

MASCARA I trumps MASCARA II.

CHAPTER 20

"Baylor Jeffries"

When Liam showed up to my house with a tall cylinder hat on his head, I had no clue what he was. Aimee was about to drive us to the dance, for which I was eternally grateful. Not only did I not have to show up with a parent, but I got to show up with a MASCARA.

"What are you?" I asked with a smirk.

"What am I? I'm a mascara!" Liam answered.

"Oh aren't you hilarious," I said. It actually was kind of hilarious. I opened the door to see the rest of him and he twirled around like a girl as we started to approach Aimee's car.

He had a make-up brand written down the side of him in what I had to admit was decent craftsmanship.

I was dressed like a 1920s flapper. It was relatively inexpensive and the little hairband kept my hair tame. Plus, I didn't care about winning any contests. I assumed there'd be at least five flappers there. There are always five flappers.

"We should have done something together," I noted.

"We did, we're both mascara's," Liam said.

"You think this is way funnier than it is."

"Oh it's *that* funny. It's people choice on the contests Jorie. I'm totally going to win for most original. It's that simple."

Liam opened the door. I ducked into the backseat. Liam sat with me like we were being chauffeured.

"It's so nice to meet you Aimee, thanks for driving us," I said.

She turned around to give me the sisterly once over.

"Oh no problem at all. Flapper?"

"Ha, how'd you guess?"

"How's MASCARA treating you?" she asked.

"It's all really new to me still. Good so far though," I said.

"I hear we have some competition. Girls starting their own sorority? How very lame of them."

Aimee looked a lot like Liam. She had a round face with even features and short blond hair. The type of angel face that you know will make a good mom someday.

"Do you know when the app will be up again?" she asked me.

"I don't. I heard a few weeks but honestly, I've never been on it. I don't even know what was on there or what was at risk."

"A lot. Basically every piece of history MASCARA has. All of our rules, all of our notes through the bidding process, our pledge tasks, everything. Tasks you never even got to."

Yikes.

I can't picture Abby as the type of person to hack into a secure app and steal information. Then again, I didn't picture Abby as the type of person to do any of the villainous things she had done this semester. For all I knew she has been a liar my whole life and I only caught on now.

"The timing is ironic. All of the drops decide to start a sorority within days of the app getting hacked. They probably wanted to know how to start a sorority in the first place," I said.

Liam looked genuinely disinterested. He was reading sports scores on his phone.

"You're probably right, but there just isn't any way to prove it yet. Hey are Asher and Mara going to pull each other's hair out for Fall Queen?"

I laughed. "I hope not. It doesn't seem like Asher would care. Mara definitely would."

I had very briefly thought about bailing on Liam. I mean, he was only "ordered" to go with me because I was pledging and pledges couldn't date. Technically, I could have bailed on Liam and gone with whomever I wanted now.

Sadly, no one asked. And the truth was, I liked Liam. He was fun to be around and understood MASCARA and his sister was great. He was also easy on the eyes.

I did have a pang of sadness whenever I thought about Derek not asking me though. I couldn't figure out why he wouldn't ask me. I thought about it over and over again. About the conversation I had overheard in the bathroom. About the fact that he knew I crossed over and could go with him now. Maybe he had heard I was going with Liam?

I wouldn't have truly bailed on Liam. I don't think. I want to believe I wouldn't have.

We walked arm-in-arm into the gym, which was filled to the brim with Halloween décor. Nothing incredibly frightening, this *was* Catholic school. They got an "A" for effort though.

I spotted Abby and Jake as soon as I walked in. They were some sort of zombie bride and zombie husband. I kept walking. She just wasn't even worth my time.

"You want eyeball punch?" Liam asked me.

"If that's a corny joke and you punch me in the eye, I will be very displeased," I said.

"No, really. It's over there."

"Sure," I said.

"Be right back."

There were tons of orange table-clothed tables with candy corn strewn over the tops of them and black folding chairs to sit. I put my bag down and walked around trying to figure out who people were underneath their masks.

I finally spotted Asher and super hot college boy who had to be Frankie. Asher was dressed like a fairy. She had striped thigh highs on and intricate wings with a bodysuit-like thing and a tutu. Definitely beat my flapper. Super hot college boy who had to be Frankie was just dressed like a super hot college boy. Too mature for a costume I guess.

"Jorie, this is Frankie. Frankie, this is Jorie," Asher said.

"I've heard a lot about you," Frankie said and shook my hand.

Really?

"Likewise," I said.

"Where's Liam?"

"Getting eyeball punch."

"Notice the lights are the same as my school dance lights in my bathroom?" Asher asked and smiled.

I looked around. They totally were.

"Yes," I laughed.

"Have you seen Derek?" Asher asked me, which was a really weird question to ask me.

I scrunched my eyebrows. "No, why?"

"Come sit with us over on that side. You can be a buffer between Mara and I in case I win Fall Queen. This way she can't punch me. I think she spent like three hundred dollars on her costume."

"What is she?"

"I have no idea," Asher said.

"I'm a guitar player, in case you couldn't guess my costume," Frankie added.

And right around then, I heard, "Frankie!"

I turned and saw a Barbie Doll heading Frankie's way. There was just no chance that this girl's costume was anything but a Barbie Doll.

"Let's go find Liam and get that punch," Asher said quickly and tugged on my arm.

I got the feeling she was trying to dodge Barbie. Too late. Barbie was now at our table, doe-eyed and hugging Frankie.

Asher gave Barbie a fake smile, so I sort of gave her a constipated smile. My fake smile was never a very good one.

Barbie put out her tiny arm filled with pink bracelets to shake my hand. I put my hand in hers.

"Hi! I'm Baylor. Jeffries. I go to school with Frankie. My boyfriend goes here. Derek Mackey," she said.

I was pretty sure someone just shot a bullet down my throat.

Asher pulled at my flapper dress.

"I'm Jorie," I said. Or at least I think I said. More like, croaked.

"Come on Jorie, Liam needs help carrying that punch," Asher urged.

I just stood there. I had something lodged so deep in my chest I couldn't move. I started to feel the stinging burn in the way, way back of my eye sockets and I knew I had to get out of there.

I looked at Asher, slowly.

"Okay," was all I said to her.

The next thing I remember was blue-streaked cheeks and wads of toilet paper. Asher was squatting in front of me desperately trying to fix my make-up but I now resembled a flapper that was buried and came back to life.

I was sobbing like a little girl and I really didn't want Asher to see that side of me.

I had no idea how long we'd been in the bathroom stall. All I knew was that Derek was dating a girl that made a better Barbie than Barbie herself.

"Did you know?" I finally asked Asher.

She half-nodded.

"Kind of. They are always breaking up. On again, off again. I didn't know they were back on. But I figured you'd get hurt either way. I tried to warn you Jor."

Asher was right. She did try to warn me. I stared at the swirls in her fairy wings. I was actually wishing on a fairy for this moment not to be real.

"You're missing the dance. You should go," I said to her.

I wiped the mascara from under my eyes and indigo lines blurred all over my cheeks.

"I don't mind missing the dance," Asher said.

"But they're gonna announce Fall Queen soon," I said between sobs.

"Oh trust me, Mara is winning that thing. I rigged so many boxes with her name."

"Why? Don't you want to win?"

"Not like she wants to win. It'll mean way more to her than it would me. Plus, she should be up there with Rob."

"Why would Adrianna tell me that he thought I was cute in the first place? Start this whole thing in my head?"

"Because you are cute. He probably does think you're cute. Why wouldn't he? Maybe that's all it was."

No. She was wrong. There was no way I had imagined all of it. The smiley-faced sticker and the stares and the almost moment. He felt something.

I picked my pretty dress up off the toilet seat and leaned to open the latch on the stall.

"I'm fine. It's fine," I said. I knew and Asher knew I wasn't even in the same family as fine but for the moment, I would pretend I was fine. My costume was fine flapper girl.

We started walking out of the stall just as zombie bride Abby was walking in with her newfound sorority.

"Just what *are* you gonna have when Asher graduates?" Abby asked. The girls laughed. They actually laughed.

"Ignore them," Asher said to me.

And I did.

We missed the crowning of Fall King and Queen. Asher was right, Mara won. Asher was also right that Mara's costume was a complete mystery. She planted a big kiss on Rob as soon as she won, which of course she thought was on her own merit.

I thought more and more about Abby's words as the dance ticked on.

What *was* I going to have when Asher graduated? I wasn't incredibly close to any of the other girls in MASCARA. I was kind of friends with Andy but I would have said I was friends with Ashley and look how well that turned out.

And now I certainly wouldn't have Derek. Imagine if I would have gotten blackballed for him? Or if my parents hadn't come ten minutes early and I had made out with him at the party? I wanted to hug my parents now for being so annoying.

Derek was just as bad as Mr. Mayer in my eyes. I hadn't seen him once tonight but that was probably a good thing. I might actually slap him, and I had never slapped a boy in the face before. I mean, I slap my brother once in a while but not in the face.

The costume prizes were being given out. Anyone with a halfway decent costume was parading around the center of the gym like a dog in a dog show. I sniffed the last of my teary episode up my nose.

And then, just like that, I knew how I could feel better.

The most original costume prize (which was $200) went to my good-looking date that I had been ignoring all night thus far. So, I decided to take one from the Mara rulebook and walk straight up to him and plant a giant kiss on his lips in front of the entire school.

Maybe it was the punch. I turned into forward flapper girl.

All I know, was it was the single best kiss I had ever had. People whistled and clapped and guys shouted things like "Go Liam!" from behind me. I whirled around after Liam and I finally unlocked lips, and locked eyes dead on Derek.

He stood, next to Baylor Barbie Jeffries, completely and utterly still.

[To Be Continued]